W9-ABQ-351

"Belle, we've got to go. This cabin will go up like a matchbox!"

Staring down at the dark hole in the floor, Belle felt her chest tighten. The idea of being alone with Jonah down there made her heart palpitate.

"Look, I'll go first." He stepped down into the hole. "See? It's a safe room with supplies and a hidden exit. We can get outside that way."

She wrung her trembling hands and shook her head. "No, no," she whimpered. "Please—"

A riotous crash from behind startled her. The kitchen window shattered, and flames licked at the ceiling and crept through to the walls. Black smoke rolled into the room.

"Belle! Listen to me. I'm an FBI agent. Come with me now!"

A deafening blast of a rifle's report boomed. Another window shattered, sending glass kernels raining down in a glittery blue shower over Belle's head. She fell to the ground and screamed...

Kate Angelo is an author, wife, minister and speaker from Missouri who works alongside her husband to strengthen and encourage marriages and families. As mom to five children, she's fluent in both sarcasm and eye rolls. With her Chihuahua taking up half her desk space and coffee at hand, Kate writes suspenseful stories of imperfect people who encounter hope and healing while ducking danger along the way. Learn more at kateangelo.com.

Books by Kate Angelo

Love Inspired Suspense

Hunting the Witness

Visit the Author Profile page at LoveInspired.com.

HUNTING THE WITNESS

KATE ANGELO

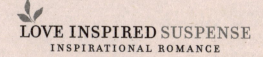

LOVE INSPIRED SUSPENSE

INSPIRATIONAL ROMANCE

If you purchased this book without a cover you should be aware that this book is stolen property. It was reported as "unsold and destroyed" to the publisher, and neither the author nor the publisher has received any payment for this "stripped book."

LOVE INSPIRED® SUSPENSE
INSPIRATIONAL ROMANCE

ISBN-13: 978-1-335-59761-8

Hunting the Witness

Copyright © 2023 by Katherine Angelo

All rights reserved. No part of this book may be used or reproduced in any manner whatsoever without written permission except in the case of brief quotations embodied in critical articles and reviews.

This is a work of fiction. Names, characters, places and incidents are either the product of the author's imagination or are used fictitiously. Any resemblance to actual persons, living or dead, businesses, companies, events or locales is entirely coincidental.

For questions and comments about the quality of this book, please contact us at CustomerService@Harlequin.com.

Love Inspired
22 Adelaide St. West, 41st Floor
Toronto, Ontario M5H 4E3, Canada
www.LoveInspired.com

Printed in U.S.A.

Recycling programs for this product may not exist in your area.

The Lord is good, a strong hold in the day of trouble;
and he knoweth them that trust in him.
—*Nahum* 1:7

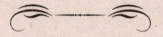

To God,
Who fills me daily with unimaginable peace and joy.

To my husband,
my prayer warrior, adviser, supporter and best friend.

ONE

Dr. Belinda Lewis found it impossible to focus on studying algae when the shadow of a serial killer lurked in her mind. She crouched at the edge of the mountain lake and used her cell phone to photograph the growing algae in her research project.

Two months ago, she'd discovered a new genus of conjugating green algae in Eagle Lake, high in the Colorado mountains. The never-before classified algae contained unusual photoprotective properties and formed striking amounts of sunscreen compounds. With her discovery and months of research, she was on the cusp of creating the first all-natural sunscreen product.

The buzz of an incoming call startled her, and she almost dropped her phone in the water. Since when did she have cell service this far into the mountains?

She stood and accepted the call. "Dr. Lewis."

"Am I speak…Dr. Bel…Lewis?" The woman's voice on the other end of the call echoed and scratched.

Belinda stole a glance at her screen. Not even one bar. No wonder the call sounded terrible. "Yes, this is Belinda Lewis, but I can barely hear you."

"I'm calling to schedule…FBI field office…"

A rustling sound came from the forest behind her. She whirled, eyes scanning the tree line. No, it couldn't be the serial killer. Probably an animal coming for a drink of water. If it was an elk or bear, she didn't want to be between them and their drink.

"Listen, I don't have much cell coverage. I'll have to call you back and schedule—"

"This isn't optional, Dr. Lewis. If you don't appear in person, you could be arrested on a material witness warrant." The woman's voice didn't skip this time but sounded metallic.

Arrested? A knot of unease formed in her stomach. "Am I... I mean, will I have to testify?"

"Because of you, that young woman is alive today. The photo...clear enough...facial recognition software... a suspect..."

"I'm having trouble hearing you. Are you still there?"

Belinda checked her screen and saw the signal had dropped. Better head home and return the call before the FBI hauled her in like a criminal instead of a witness. All because she happened to interrupt a man attacking a woman. Of course, she was too far away to do anything other than yell and take a blurry picture, but apparently it was all the FBI needed to identify the attacker as a suspected serial killer.

With a sigh, she slipped her phone and research journal into her backpack and double-checked the can of bear spray clipped to the shoulder strap. The gravel crunched under her boots as she headed away from the lake toward the trailhead. She climbed the steep path and paused at the top of the bluff to take in the breathtaking view of Eagle Lake. Views like this were one reason she'd moved out of the city and into her home near the base of the mountain.

Halfway to her car, she heard a faint rumble from the south. The reverberation rolled like thunder, then faded.

Despite the blistering summer sun beating down through the trees, she shivered. Took a deep breath and let it out little by little. Probably a short morning storm on the other side of the mountain. Happened all the time. She slowed her steps and surveyed the forest. Her nerves pricked with the uncanny sense of a shadow lurking nearby.

A branch snapped.

She twisted and scanned the area in the direction of the noise but saw nothing. Ever since the incident with the suspected serial killer the news had dubbed the "Trail-side Strangler," her paranoia was over the top. She had to relax. The wilderness was full of noises, and she couldn't let each one cause her to jump out of her skin. Besides, her heart didn't appreciate the constant adrenaline surge.

A shadow drifted behind a thicket of trees in her peripheral. Belinda stilled.

Tree limbs cracked and a rapid thudding reverberated against the forest floor. The rhythmic sound grew louder and louder.

Before she could make sense of what she heard, branches swayed and broke apart. Frozen, she stared horrified as a massive elk crashed through the trees. His wide antlers scraped the trees as he galloped onto the trail, headed right for her.

Belinda's body seized in anticipation of the impact. She sucked in a sharp breath.

At the last second, the elk noticed her and changed course. The mammoth animal bounded past in a gush of wind.

Belinda let out a breath and watched the elk disappear into the forest. She pressed her eyes closed and took long breaths until she slowed her pulse.

An elk nearly trampled her on the trail. Oh sure, she'd been in sight of a serial killer, but an elk? Now that was real danger. She chuckled. Was there a more ridiculous way to die?

A snort escaped and soon she was laughing at the idea of a newscaster telling the world an elk squashed a phycologist, and then explaining that *phycologist* meant algae scientist. The giggles took over until she gasped for breath and wiped tears from her eyes.

Still laughing, she turned and slammed into the hard chest of a bear. No, a man the size of a grizzly.

Surprise came out in a high-pitched gasp, and she took two steps back. The man dressed in hunting camouflage towered over her. Black eyes glared beneath the brim of his baseball cap.

"Oh! I'm so sorry." Her heart thumped against her chest. "I—I wasn't watching where I—"

A slow sneer spread across his face.

His tree trunk of an arm shot out and grabbed her neck. The big hands squeezed Belinda's throat and his massive thumbs pressed into her windpipe. Her mind grappled to understand her situation, even as he lifted her feet off the ground.

Instinct told her to fight. Fight him off. Whatever the cost, don't stop fighting. She dug her nails into his thick fingers and wrenched at his hold on her throat. No matter how hard she strained, his grip wouldn't loosen. She fumbled for her bear spray. Managed to brush it with her fingertips but couldn't quite grasp it. Pulsing white spots danced in her vision.

He was going to kill her.

A wave of panic mounted. She could not pass out. She flailed, kicking and swinging her arms wildly. Her hand found his nose, and she clawed at his face. Tried to get his DNA under her nails in case…in case…

No. She would *not* let him win.

Determination spiked, and she fought harder. Her hand connected with the brim of his hat and sent it sailing to the ground. His black eyes narrowed, and she searched them for meaning behind this attack, but only found emptiness.

But there was *something* about those eyes...

Recognition flared, and she tried to scream, but only managed a guttural groan. His grip loosened a fraction as he lowered her. Her feet touched earth and with trembling legs, she managed to stand upright. Her windpipe opened, and she inhaled slivers of lifesaving oxygen.

"You," she said in a hoarse whisper. "It's...you."

The corner of his lip curled. "I found you, Belinda."

The blood in her veins turned to ice and realization shot through her entire body. He was toying with her. Cutting off precious oxygen to bring her to the edge of death then loosening his grip to bring her back again. He *would* kill her if she didn't get away. Eventually.

With self-defense training, she had the moves to escape an attacker. If only she could remember. Wait. She did remember.

Muscle memory took over. Alligator neck. She stiffened every muscle from her shoulders to her head and tucked her chin to her chest as far as his hands would allow. In one quick motion, she stepped back with her right foot and bowed her head. With balled fists she prepared to strike. She ducked between his arms and twisted her body away.

Unable to fight her momentum, he let her slip from his grasp. She ran, but barely managed three steps before she was yanked aside by her backpack and fell. She scrambled to her feet and slipped out of the straps. He dropped the bag and lunged for her, but she pivoted on her opposite heel and sprinted away.

Her hands went to her neck, and she rubbed her throat. Tried to get her windpipe to open again. Every breath made her cough, but she tried to suppress it so the sound wouldn't give her away.

"Belinda…" His raspy voice drew her name out. "There's nowhere to go, Belinda."

Heavy footfalls pounded the earth close on her heels.

She darted between trees, her hands raised to block the foliage. A low branch slashed her face and a line of warm blood trickled down her cheek. Her shoe caught a rock and she stumbled two steps, then fell on her palms. Pain shot through her wrists, but she scrambled to her feet. Move. Keep moving.

Only a few yards between them.

With an angry snarl, the attacker lunged and caught her T-shirt. Instinct drove her to the ground, and she scurried between his legs. The fabric tore, but she got to her feet with enough time to bolt through the trees.

She ignored the sting of her wounds and searched for signs of the trail so she could get to her car. Her stomach sank. The car keys were in her backpack. The phone too. She should've clipped the bear spray to her waist instead of her backpack. Now the lake was her only hope, and she prayed someone else would be there.

A noise from behind made her whip her head around. He was there, but farther in the distance, losing speed. All her weekend hikes and hours at the gym were paying off as she outran her attacker.

She hurdled a fallen tree and zig-zagged her way through a bramble bush until her calves burned with the uphill climb. A stitch in her side caused her to gasp and clutch her waist, but she couldn't stop now. She had to make it to the lake and find help.

Belinda skirted a crevasse and headed for the tree

with a split trunk she recognized from her past hikes.
She was higher than she realized and if she remembered
correctly that tree was atop the bluff north of the trail.
She'd gone too far. Now she needed to get to the ridge
and see if help was near the lake.

She lunged over a boulder in the path and reached out
to brace herself on a nearby tree. The mountainous frame
of her attacker appeared with a cruel smile on his lips.

Belinda screamed.

A bloodcurdling scream yanked Jonah's attention from
the trout on his line. The shrill cry echoed across the valley and kicked his pulse into high gear. Special Agent
Jonah Phillips had been with the FBI long enough to
recognize the cry of someone in trouble, and that shriek
came from one terrified woman.

Jonah tossed his rod on the ground beside the creek
and grabbed his rifle. He scrambled his way up the slop-
ing bank. His rubber boots slipped on the mud and wet
rocks. Several times, he lost his footing and almost fell.
The waders and attached boots were not at all built for
climbing. A gnarled tree root protruded from the ledge,
and he used it to pull himself over. At the edge of the
bank, he paused and considered which way to go.

The woman had to be on the trail near the cold-water
lake that fed the creek where his fish now made its escape. Jonah bolted in the direction of the cry, mindful of
the small round stones protruding from the narrow dirt
path. One wrong step could result in a nasty fall.

He strained to hear over the swish of his rubber waders. Whoever screamed would surely do it again, wouldn't
she? If the woman was hurt, she would cry out for help
until someone came. But Jonah was sure what he heard
wasn't a cry for help. It was pure terror. One long scream

cut off abruptly. With his rifle in both hands and pointed skyward, he picked up the pace.

He burst from the forest into a clearing and the mountain lake came into view. The thin air caused him to pant harder than usual, but he couldn't afford to pause and catch his breath. It could cost the woman her life.

After two weeks living full-time in his vacation cabin, he still wasn't acclimated to the elevation. The assistant director had pulled Jonah from his undercover operation and ordered him to take an off-grid vacation. A mix-up in another case put his months of working to infiltrate a drug cartel at risk, and Jonah couldn't afford to be seen in public.

But he couldn't let a woman die, either.

Hands on his hips, he surveyed the knee-high wildflowers and the edge of the lake. Mountains and fluffy white clouds reflected off the still water. The craggy hiking trail snaked down the side of the mountain directly across the lake. There was no one in sight. The woman must be higher.

He had to get over there, but that meant finding a way to the other side of the small lake. To his left was a shorter path, but he'd have to navigate wet rocks and boulders that would surely slow him down. It was summer, but the glacier runoff meant the lake was frigid. If he fell into the icy water, he'd be the one in need of a rescue.

The trail on the right meandered off into another wooded area that led to a scenic overlook before circling back to the lake. Which direction had the cry come from? If he chose the wrong path, the woman could die before he reached her.

Heavy grunts echoed across the lake along with the rustle of foliage. His eyes darted along the tree line until he saw movement on the bluff. The outline of a man in camouflage wavered near a tree. Hunting wasn't allowed in this area, but it wasn't rare for a tourist tracking a bear or mountain lion to get lost. Maybe it was a woman chased to the lake by an animal and now she needed help. But where was she?

"Hey!" Jonah shouted. "Anybody there? Do you need help?"

His voice bounced off the rocks and echoed in three soft waves before it went quiet again. No reply. He reached for his phone to call the park ranger but didn't find it.

Jonah groaned. He wasn't on duty; he was on sabbatical. He'd left his phone at the cabin for some peace. Besides, it never had coverage around here, anyway.

The branches swayed uphill, and two limbs parted for a second, giving Jonah a view. Two figures struggled near a huge oak tree at the top of the ridge. A dark-haired man dressed in camouflage pants and jacket towered over a woman, his back to Jonah. They swayed and stumbled, stepping closer to the cliff. If they weren't careful, they'd fall right off the edge.

Jonah yelled. "Hey! Let her go!"

Camouflage Man turned to peer at Jonah over his shoulder. Jonah tried to make out his features, but he was too far away. The man clutched the woman by the throat. Her feet dangled off the ground, the tips of her toes stretched toward solid earth. She grappled with Camouflage Man's immense hands, but clearly his grip was strong. Was it possible this was the Trailside Strangler?

He didn't have time to consider it. The woman needed help, and he was a hundred yards away with a lake between them.

Jonah shouldered his rifle and took aim. "FBI! Put your hands where I can see them!"

Camouflage Man dragged the woman closer to the

edge of the cliff. Jonah's heart slammed against his chest. It was at least a twenty-foot drop on the rocky slope. If she fell...

He had to get to the other side of the lake before it was too late.

Even though he didn't have a clean shot, Jonah kept his weapon trained on the man, looking away long enough to place his feet. He climbed over slick boulders and slogged his way through the knee-high water. The cold stole his breath, and he was thankful the waders kept him dry. The burn of mountain-air pricked his lungs with each breath, but he pressed on.

When he was halfway to the bank, he assessed the situation again. The attacker still held the woman in front of him and blocked Jonah's shot, holding her like a hostage.

They were on the edge of the ridge, only a few inches from a deadly fall.

The woman sagged in the big man's hands. Had she passed out? Or worse? He kept going, closing the distance, but too far away to save the woman. He clenched his rifle, itching to pull the trigger.

"This is the FBI," Jonah shouted. "Show me your hands!"

The man stared at Jonah and cocked his head. For a moment, Jonah thought he would comply. With one quick movement, Camouflage Man flung the woman over the edge of the cliff. Before Jonah could take a shot, the attacker ducked behind a tree and disappeared.

The woman's body slid feetfirst along the bluff. Her hands grappled for a hold, but only found loose gravel. Halfway down the slope, her foot hit a protruding tree root. Her feet went over her head, and she tumbled twice, bringing larger rocks raining down the precipice with her. She hit the ground hard on her hip. The momentum kept her going and she flipped and landed with a splash on the shore of the lake.

Jonah clenched his jaw and kept his eye on the crumpled body of the woman, now lying motionless in the frigid water. If he didn't get to her soon, she'd either freeze or drown. With his rifle lowered, he climbed a boulder and took a risky leap toward the bank. Before he could plant his left foot, it slipped. He fell, landing hard against the rock. A sharp pain shot through his side, but he ignored it and got to his feet.

He slogged through the mud at the edge of the lake and dropped to his knees next to the woman. Blood tinted the water surrounding her cinnamon-colored curls. Wow, she was small. Tiny actually. No more than five feet and probably all of one hundred pounds soaking wet. Which she was. He had to get her out of the water.

He laid his rifle on the ground and leaned over to check her vitals. A smooth rock beneath her cheek supported her head. A slight ripple skittered across the water near her mouth with each shallow breath.

Breathing…breathing was good.

With his free hand, he felt her throat for a pulse. It was slow but strong against his fingers. His shoulders relaxed and he heaved a sigh. She was unconscious, not dead. Bits of gravel clung to her cheek. Jonah brushed them away.

He looked around and considered what to do next. A fall from such a height meant she probably had a head or neck injury. Moving her could cause more damage, but what choice did he have? The glacier runoff water would send her into hypothermia in minutes, and what if her attacker came back while Jonah went for help? No, he'd risk moving her to save her life.

Gently, he lifted her and cradled her in his arms. "It's okay," he whispered. "I've got you."

He carried her to a dry patch of grass where the sun shone through the trees and lowered her to the ground. When he brought his hand away from her hair, blood stained his fingers.

The skin near her temple had burst open. Blood trickled down her face. The cut looked bad, but it wasn't life-threatening. She'd definitely need stitches. He tore the corner of his flannel shirt and applied pressure to staunch the bleeding.

The woman moaned, then coughed. Her eyes fluttered, but she didn't open them.

"It's okay. You're safe. Can you tell me your name?" He stroked her hair, hoping the stimulation would rouse her.

She pulled her cracked lips apart. "B-b-b…" Her voice was nothing more than a shallow breath.

"It's okay. Take your time." Jonah's eyes drifted to the finger shaped bruises already appearing around her neck.

"B-b-bel…"

"Belle? Your name is Belle?"

She didn't respond.

"Okay, we'll go with that for now." He blew out a breath. "Sorry we had to meet like this, Belle, but I'll get you somewhere safe."

She seemed stable, but there was no doubt this woman needed medical attention. Without his phone, he'd have to carry her to his cabin before he could call the ranger station for help.

He lifted her slight body and settled her into his arms.

Jonah's boss was not going to like this. This was the opposite of laying low. The authorities needed to know about the attack and take Jonah's witness statement. Which meant he'd have to explain why he was in the vicinity. Only his handler knew the location of his secret cabin. No other human had ever set foot in it.

Footsteps scuffled closer. "Here, let's prop you up so you can take a drink," a man's voice said. He tucked another pillow behind her head.

She flinched at the object that brushed her lips. The edge of a cup. Chilled liquid touched her mouth. She shouldn't accept a drink from a stranger, but her thirst overpowered logic.

Her lips cracked as she pursed them in anticipation. Cool water moistened her tongue, and a sense of satisfaction she'd never known overwhelmed her. She sucked in more, desperate for the soothing sensation to continue. When her mouth was full, she tried to swallow, but her throat was raw. A coughing fit sent the water sputtering.

"Take it easy," the deep voice soothed.

A hot tear rolled from the corner of her eye. Why did everything hurt so bad? Not only her throat but her head. The steady throbbing of her pulse beat a rhythm in her ears and sounded like a snare drum.

Water. She needed more water. Clumsily, she reached for the cup and her fingers knocked into it. Sandbags weighed her arms. Every limb heavy and refusing to cooperate.

"Don't try to move," the man said. "You fell and hit your head rather hard. Probably have a concussion."

The cup was at her lips again and out of desperation, she took another long pull. Most of it managed to slide down before she coughed. Liquid dribbled from the corner of her mouth and the man wiped it with his rough thumb.

"Easy," he said. "I know you're thirsty but let's take it slow. If you drink too quickly you could choke."

Choke.

The word sent a jolt of lightning through her heart. A vague memory appeared like a vapor. A man in the woods. Camouflage and black eyes. Thick fingers around her neck. Squeezing… Choking… Can't…breathe…

"Hey, hey now," the man soothed. "You're okay. You're safe." He helped her into a sitting position and leaned her against a headboard. He turned and carried the drink away.

She tried to see the man, but her eyelids were heavy and she only managed to keep them open a blink at a time. *Blink.* A ratty blue-and-red quilt covered her legs. Not in a hospital. *Blink.* A ceiling pitched upward and brought the center of the room to a peak. *Blink.* Hand-hewn beams supported the structure. She was in a house.

Dizziness made her feel sick, and she didn't dare move too fast. Her eyes still burned, but she surveyed the rest of the room. The metal-framed bed where she lay filled one corner of the cabin. A round wooden table served double duty as a nightstand and an end table to the beat-up leather recliner. Bright beams of sunlight streamed through the three windows along the top of each of the four walls of the cabin. A stone fireplace with a mounted elk head over the mantel anchored the room.

In the kitchen area, an ancient wood-burning stove glowed with a fire behind its cast-iron door. A tall man worked at the kitchen counter with his back to her. He hummed to himself as he moved between the counter and the sink.

"Where…where am I?" Needles stabbed her throat.

The man turned at the sound of her voice. Something in his hand glinted in the light. The blade of a knife.

Blackness clouded her vision and her stomach lurched. The attacker had caught her. Brought her here to torture her before killing her. A sob rose and she thought she might be sick. She tried to get out of bed, but weakness overtook her muscles.

The man hurried to catch her before she fell. "Hold on there. I think you better rest a while longer before you try to move."

She leaned into the pillows. His thumb caressed her arm in slow circles. Gentle and kindly. The sensation soothed her. Her head began to clear. The pain eased.

But no. He was the reason she was here. She was his prisoner.

"No," she whimpered and pulled her arm away. Wrapped it around her waist. Too weak to do anything more.

She squeezed her lids closed, unable to look her attacker in the eyes. Tears rolled over her cheeks and trickled into her ears. This had to be a dream. If only she could wake. But it wasn't a dream. It was a nightmare.

The man moved and she sensed him hovering over her. She snapped her eyes open and tensed for the blow sure to come, but he didn't hit her. Instead, he reached across the bed and grabbed a pillow, bringing it toward her head.

"No!" She held her hands out, ready to block his attempt to smother her face.

His eyes went wide. He looked at the pillow in his hand. Dropped it and held his palms out. "Oh, no… Hey, I'm not gonna hurt you. I'm sorry. I didn't mean to scare you."

The mattress sank under his weight when he sat on the edge of the bed near her feet. "My name is Jonah. I was out fishing when I heard you scream. Someone attacked you and I found you by the lake. You're pretty banged up, but nothing too serious. How do you feel?"

She lifted a shoulder in response and studied his face. He had messy black hair in need of a haircut and a full beard covering most of his face. At least he seemed to keep it neat and trimmed. But there was something in his dark eyes… A familiarity that caused her adrenaline to spike.

"Here, have some tea." He reached for the mug on the nightstand. "The honey should help soothe your throat."

He held the cup and she sipped, watching him over the rim. The warm tea eased the soreness, and she was grateful. With her eyes fixed on his, she took in every feature of the man. He said his name was Jonah and he rescued her. But was he the man who attacked her? She couldn't remember. If he was the attacker, why was he being so nice?

A tear slipped out. She wanted to ask questions. How long had she been here, and why wasn't she in a hospital? When she opened her mouth to speak, she only managed a whimper.

"It's okay," he soothed. "I'm not gonna hurt you. You're safe now." Jonah ran his calloused fingers over her cheek and wiped the stray tear away.

Alarm bells clanged inside her head. She wasn't *safe*.

This man was a killer and the whole thing was some deranged act designed to keep her calm before the real torture began. But she was in too much pain to run away. At this point she might pass out if she tried to stand. No, she would gather her strength and at the first opportunity make her escape.

He offered the tea again, but she lifted a hand and waved him off. "Where…am…I?"

"This is my…" He paused and shifted his eyes. "It's my hunting cabin."

The way he said *hunting* cabin sounded ominous. Did he hunt people and bring them here?

When she didn't respond he continued, "You were hiking near Eagle Lake when you were attacked."

"Eagle Lake?" The name was familiar, but she couldn't place it.

"It's the nearest lake to my cabin. I sometimes fish there. Don't you remember?"

She shook her head. Bad idea. A wave of nausea overcame her, and bile rose in her throat.

She stared at Jonah. "I...I... I'm going to be sick."

With all his FBI training, Jonah could handle just about anything. Anything but vomit.

Sure, he'd been trained to field-dress wounds and keep a person alive as long as possible, but cleaning human sick? No way.

The woman he now held in his arms threw up on his braided wool rug then fainted. At least he'd been quick enough to grab her before she hit the floor. The last thing this poor woman needed was another bump on her head.

He leaned the petite woman against the pillows and nestled the blanket around her waist. The pinkish-red bruises contrasted against her fair skin and the sight of them caused his temper to flare. He'd cleaned the dirt from her freckled face and bandaged the cut on her temple when he brought her home, but traces of dirt clung to the tips her wild red curls.

He filled a bowl with warm water and sat on the edge of the bed. Dabbing the washcloth in the liquid, he cleaned her face, taking extra care around the smaller cuts. He wiped the dirt from her hair. A stray curl stuck to her bandage. He eased it out and tucked it behind her ear. Already she was looking and smelling a bit better.

Now for the rug. He rolled it up and carted it to the deck outside and draped it over the railing. It would take a long soak in vinegar to eliminate the smell, but a quick rinse would do for now. Using a bucket, he poured soapy water over the rug and wiped it with the washcloth. He rinsed it twice and left it hanging on the rail to dry.

Jonah stretched his long arms over his head and studied the tree line. The forest beyond his front yard seemed eerily silent. None of the usual animal noises. Quiet like this only happened when a predator lurked nearby.

Watching the trees for movement, he thought about the day's events. He was supposed to be laying low, staying out of sight while his handler, Special Agent in Charge Chase Bishop, worked to clear his name. A sabbatical they'd called it. A little R & R in his hunting cabin while they "straightened things out."

Well, laying low wasn't an option. The woman—did she say her name was Belle? He'd have to ask when she woke again. She needed medical attention. X-rays, a brain scan and maybe more. All of which required going into town and showing his face. Yeah, Chase would *not* be happy.

Jonah studied a shadowy patch of trees. A leafy branch swayed upward, and he tensed. Alert for any sign of Camouflage Man, Jonah stilled himself and waited. The branch swayed again, and Jonah caught sight of a chipmunk scurrying along the tree limb. He blew out a breath. Silly animal.

The hair prickled on Jonah's neck. The pressure in the air seemed different. Somewhere out there, evil lurked. A serial killer.

Women disappeared from remote areas of the Rocky Mountain National Park only to have their bodies discovered by hikers weeks later. Some not far from Jonah's own cabin. One reporter called the suspect the *Trailside Strangler* and the name spread like wildfire, but Jonah thought the moniker was ridiculous. His opinion didn't matter. It wasn't his case, but it was the reason he was stuck here instead of in his undercover assignment where he belonged.

He took a long look and headed inside.

Work files in hand, he plopped into his recliner and put his feet up. He might be on forced sabbatical, but he wasn't about to stop being an FBI agent. Not when he'd spent months to infiltrate a drug cartel at the highest level. So with not much else to do, he'd spent hours poring over the case files. He knew them inside and out. Read and reread the transcripts of his taped conversations. He wanted to be prepared to return to his undercover life as soon as possible.

His eyes drifted to Belle asleep in his bed. Her chest rose and fell with deep, even breaths. How had she survived the attack? A man twice her size strangled her then flung her over the bluff like trash. If Jonah had been there a few minutes earlier, he might have saved her. But what if he hadn't been there at all? Jonah shook his head and gritted his teeth. No one should treat another human with such hatred.

But who was the attacker? An angry ex-boyfriend or the serial killer lurking in the woods? The Trailside Strangler had never picked a victim from this area. Only left the bodies.

Whoever he was, he'd made a big mistake by attacking this woman. Jonah would put the full weight of the FBI behind finding the guy.

Belle moaned and tossed her head, eyes squeezed shut. Her breathing picked up and each intake of breath came with a soft cry. Another bad dream. When she turned her head away, he glimpsed the bruises on her neck and seethed. He closed the file folder and set it aside. She stirred again and he moved to sit beside her. The bed gave way under his weight and jostled her, but she didn't open her eyes.

"No…" she whimpered.

The sound of her soft cry stirred his heart, and he knew the trauma she suffered would cause nightmares for a long time. "Shh, it's okay. You're safe," he said.

She tossed her head, more violently this time. Red splotches appeared on her cheeks, and she clenched her fists. Her head thrashed and she flailed her arms, fighting off an imaginary attacker. "Off! Get off!"

The nightmare worsened and he couldn't bear to watch her suffer. He nudged her shoulder. "Hey, it's okay. Wake up. You're having a bad dream."

Her sharp fingernails connected with the skin on his forearms, and he winced. Oh, she was a fighter, even in her sleep. He shook her again and spoke softly. "Wake up—you're dreaming."

The grimace on her face smoothed and her eyes popped open. Intense sky-blue eyes gazed at him. "What— Oh, my head hurts so bad."

She reached to grab her head and he caught her hands. "Easy, you have a cut on your temple right there."

He let go of her hands and she hesitated, then planted a light touch on her head. Her fingers found the bandage and brushed over it. "How?"

"You, uh." He cleared his throat, unsure if his words would upset her. "You were attacked and pushed. Banged your head pretty hard when you fell. I took care of that cut with some Steri-Strips, but I'm no doctor." He offered a weak smile.

She flicked her eyes around the room.

"Besides the cut above your eye, are you hurting anywhere else? Anything broken?"

Her gaze returned to his and she blinked a few times. Did she even hear a word he said? Probably still in shock.

"Listen, you've been through a lot. You're probably exhausted and scared, and you need medical attention. I can take you to the hospital, but I heard on my weather radio there was a landslide earlier today. The roads in this area were covered."

He scratched his beard and watched Belle's face to ensure she was listening.

"The rumble earlier," she rasped.

"You remember hearing it, good. Piney Village is about ten miles from here, but the main road is also covered. We could take my ATV, but with a head injury like yours, I'm not sure you can handle the rough drive."

"Piney…Village?"

"Yeah, you know it?"

"I… I don't think so." She fixed her stare at a spot over his shoulder. "I…think I can make it. I need to move around a bit first. Got anything for the pain?"

"Of course." He reached for the first aid kit. "Any allergies?"

"I—I don't think so…" Her voice trailed off.

He offered a cup of water and two pills. "Ibuprofen? Will that work?"

She nodded and took the pills. "Was it you?"

"Was what—oh, you think—no, I didn't attack you. I was fishing nearby and heard you scream so I came to help, that's all."

She placed the medicine in her mouth and eyed him over the rim of the glass as she washed them down. When the water was gone, she handed the cup to him. "If you aren't the man who attacked me, who are you?"

The feisty question caught him off guard and he suppressed a grin. He didn't bother telling her he'd already introduced himself. "I'm Jonah." He offered his hand to her.

She took it with a surprisingly firm grip. "Jonah." A

slight smile played at her lips, and she squinted. "And you're *sure* you're not the one who attacked me?"

A snort of laughter escaped. Boy, she was a sassy one. Even after falling down the mountain and cracking her head open, she seemed stronger than her small frame conveyed.

"Quite the opposite I assure you. But I've been taking care of you all day and I'm not sure I know *your* name."

"My name is… My name…" The amusement in her features twisted into confusion. "I… I don't know my name."

THREE

She didn't know her own name? How could she not know her own name? She blinked and stared at the man sitting on the side of her bed. There was a softness to his features that gave her a sense of security even though her entire world was flipped upside down. And yet, as she studied him a wave of panic rose, and a voice inside screamed for her to run.

Jonah furrowed his brows. "Are you telling me you don't know your own name?"

"My name? Of course, I know my name. It's, um…" Her eyes lost focus and she fumbled for the word. Why couldn't she remember? She chewed her bottom lip.

"Is it Belle?"

Belle? The name didn't feel right. Close but…not quite. The word was there, but out of reach. "No, I don't think so. But I—I don't remember."

She searched Jonah's dark eyes for any hint of malice. He seemed like a nice guy. A knight in shining armor even. He'd rescued her from danger and spent the day nursing her to health. But was it all a game? Had he drugged her? There were drugs that would cause a person to black out and wake without a memory of the past several hours. Was her memory loss nothing more than a side effect?

Her gaze flicked to the water cup, then to Jonah. "Why do you think my name is Belle?"

"You were barely conscious when I found you, but I asked your name. You mumbled something that sounded like Belle, but then you passed out."

"Belle." She tried the name but nothing.

"Besides," he said, rubbing his neck, "this is a little like a fairy tale, don't you think?"

"What?" Her voice cracked and a twinge of pain stabbed behind her eyes.

"I mean," Jonah chuckled. "A pretty woman injured in the woods, brought back to the beastly man's castle—"

"And held captive!" She fisted the blanket and pulled it to her chin.

"Wait—what? No!"

"Isn't it what you're doing? Holding me captive?" This man was playing mind games with her. First, he tried to strangle her, and now pretended to be her rescuer. Sick. He was sick.

"No, no." He showed her his palms. "You can leave anytime you want. I only brought you here to give you first aid and to protect you."

Repulsion churned in her stomach. What was happening? Should she trust this stranger or was it all some twisted game?

The glimmer of a man in hunting camouflage flashed in her memory. Did the man have a beard like Jonah? She tried to hold on to the vision, but it slipped away.

"Hang on, you said you brought me here to protect me. Does that mean you saw my attacker?"

"I saw a man in camouflage choking you. I didn't get a look at his face. Too far away. Did you?"

The image of a big man sneering popped into her head, but his face wasn't clear. It was like a dream where she sensed the person, but all the details were vague. "It's fuzzy, and when I try to picture his face, all I see is… is you."

"It's perfectly normal to have temporary memory loss and confusion with a head injury like yours. You're probably getting mixed-up. Don't worry about it right now. The important thing is you're safe."

But *was* she safe?

"Meanwhile, since you can't remember your name, I'll keep calling you Belle, if that's okay with you?"

She nodded absently, trying to remember the details of the attack. No matter how hard she tried, a black cloud hovered over the memory. Everything was right in front of her, yet she couldn't grasp it any more than she could reach out and grab a shadow. How could she trust Jonah if she couldn't remember what happened?

"How long have I been here?" She scanned his face, watching for microexpressions for indications of deceit.

"I would say—" he turned to look over his shoulder at the clock on the wall "—it's been about four hours."

It was still light outside, so early afternoon. "Why haven't you called the police or an ambulance?"

"No cell coverage out here and—"

"Wait! Did I have a phone?"

He shook his head. "Sorry, I didn't see one. No purse or wallet either."

Overwhelming disappointment clawed its way out of her gut and into her throat. What an impossible situation. No memory and no identity.

Jonah seemed nice and gentle. Maybe even attractive if he didn't have the bushy beard. But his eyes were all too familiar. The situation wasn't right. Why hadn't he called someone for help? Her chest burned as her pulse thrummed. She could hear her heartbeat in her ears. There had to be a way out of here.

"Are you okay?" he asked.

His question startled her. "I—I have to go to the bathroom."

"Oookay," he drew out the word. "I hate to tell you this, but all I've got is an outhouse."

"Fine. It's fine. I can make it."

"Are you sure?"

"Yeah, I'll just take it slow." Or fast. As soon as she got outside, she'd make a run for it.

Jonah helped her stand and guided her by the elbow to the door. A skull-crushing ache filled her head and for a moment she wondered how far she could make it. It didn't matter. She had to try. Had to escape.

Jonah grabbed his rifle on the way outside.

"What do you need that for?" she asked.

"Predators. You don't step foot outside without a gun around here. It's the only way to survive a bear or mountain lion attack. Or worse, being trampled by an elk."

Trampled by an elk? Hadn't she heard that before? It wasn't important; leaving this place was the concern.

She stepped outside and scanned the area. A small clearing surrounded by forest on all sides. All she had to do was make it to the trees and she could disappear. She'd escaped the attacker once. She could do it again.

The sun streaked through the branches; patches of light radiated through in long yellow beams that captured her curiosity. Glancing around, she didn't see any other homes. They were alone out here, which meant she'd be on her own until she found someone to help.

Belle spotted the older model Ford pickup parked away from the cabin in what passed for a driveway. Two tire tracks leading through a small opening in the trees. It

looked more like a hiking trail than a road. She eyed the truck. Were the keys in it? Should she risk checking, or head straight for the forest?

"The bathroom is right over there." Jonah pointed to a small wood building in the shape of an outhouse behind the cabin. "Are you sure you can make it that far?"

She glared at him. "Well, I'm not about to go right here."

"I didn't mean…never mind. You can sit on the steps while I do a quick check for critters. The last thing you need is a raccoon surprising you in there."

"I'd rather stand." Being on her feet would give her a head start and, in her condition, she needed every advantage. "But you should take your time. It's not an emergency and outhouses are scary enough without visitors."

Jonah nodded and trotted down the steps. She noticed his darting glances on the way to the outhouse. He seemed to be checking more than the building.

When Jonah reached for the door, she took her chance. Down the steps and away from the house, she made a beeline for the pickup. If he was like most mountain men, the keys would be somewhere inside.

After only a few steps her knees went weak, and she stumbled. *No, not now.* She had to find the strength. Her legs wobbled and she concentrated on each step. One foot in front of another. *Don't fall.* When she reached the truck, she leaned against the hood and took a moment to steady herself.

"Belle? What are you doing?" Jonah called.

Her head snapped around. Jonah walked toward her, his rifle over his shoulder. She dived for the door handle and jerked. Nothing. She yanked again and again, but the latch refused to give. Locked.

The other door. She had to try the other door. She re-

traced her steps and skirted around to the front of the truck. Her toe caught a rock, and she pitched forward. Staggered two quick steps. Stumbled, and caught herself.

Crouched beside the bumper, she glanced at Jonah. Almost to her. She had to move. She straightened and placed her hands on the hood for balance.

A deafening blast of a gun report boomed. The windshield shattered sending glass kernels raining down in a glittery blue shower over her head. She fell to the ground and screamed.

Jonah spun on his heel and sprinted toward the pickup. Belle knelt on the ground. Her fingers curled around the front bumper for support. He shouldered his rifle and searched for the shooter in the woods as he ran to her. What was Belle thinking? The truck was in the opposite direction of the outhouse. But then, what was *he* thinking leaving her standing out in the open like that?

A second gun blast shattered the passenger side mirror. A third ricocheted off the metal frame. Belle shrieked and covered her head with both hands. Jonah dropped into a crouch and returned fire, aiming into the forest but without a target in his sights. He fired three shots and covered the distance to Belle.

Dropping to his knees beside her he asked, "Are you okay?"

She nodded frantically.

Jonah peeked around the pickup. Still no sign of the gunman. They were in trouble. The shooter had a clear vantage point from the trees and while the truck provided some cover, the attacker could move in on them quickly. The deer rifle in his hand only held ten rounds and didn't have the precision or range of his larger caliber gun, the one he used for elk hunting. Jonah had to get Belle inside and get to his other weapons.

Belle whimpered and he turned to see her entire body trembling. With one arm he pulled her close. "It's okay. I've got you."

"I—I fell."

"It doesn't matter. Can you walk?"

"But someone is shooting at us."

"Yeah, I noticed. We have to get inside. On my count, run to the cabin and get inside. Don't look back. I'll cover you and be right behind you."

Her face hardened and he saw the determination in her eyes. "Okay." She angled herself in the direction of the cabin and nodded.

"You sure you can make it?"

"Being shot at helped. My head is clear now. I can do this."

He studied her for a moment then shouldered his rifle. He mouthed the countdown.

One...two...three...

Jonah rose to his feet and fired into the woods in the general direction of the gunman. Belle darted to the porch and up the steps. He was close behind, taking the steps two at a time. A bullet hit the deck railing beside him. Shards of wood splintered. He twisted and took one last shot before he crossed the threshold and slammed the front door.

Belle stood in the middle of the room hugging herself. Breaths coming fast. "Did you see him?"

Jonah peered out the window near the front door. "No, but I can tell you right now, that guy is a terrible shot. He could have picked me off at the top of the steps, but he missed."

"Or he's trying to scare us." There was hope behind her words.

"Possible, but I doubt anyone would go through the

trouble. Are you sure you can't remember who attacked you?"

If he had to guess, her attacker followed them to the cabin and hid in the forest, waiting to take his shot. The thought infuriated him. This was supposed to be his own personal safe house, and now it was under attack.

Her arms fell and she flopped into his recliner. "Everything's all fuzzy. The memories are there, but not." She blew out an audible breath and glanced at him. "I thought *you* were the man who attacked me."

"Oh, is that what you were doing? Trying to run away from me?"

The corners of her mouth tipped up. "Well, yeah. But the truck was locked, and I guess I'm still a little weak."

Jonah continued to watch the trees beyond his bullet-riddled truck for signs of the gunman. So far, no movement. "We need to call the park ranger and have them send someone out here to investigate. I'll try my satellite phone."

"Wait, why haven't you used it to call for help until right now?"

"The phone only works when there's a clear view of the sky. Out here, the trees tend to block the signal. I tried a few times without success."

He retrieved his phone from the kitchen and pointed it at her. "Stay put while I try again."

Jonah glanced at Belle and saw her staring at her hands folded in her lap The petite woman somehow appeared even smaller sitting with her feet curled under herself in his ratty old recliner. His words were too harsh, and he'd hurt her feelings.

"I'm sorry," he breathed. "I'm not used to taking care of anyone but myself."

"A loner, are you?" She chuckled. "Never would've guessed."

He snorted. "I suppose I deserve that." He crossed the room and squatted in front of her. "I've been alone out here, and I haven't talked to anyone in a while. I'm a bit rusty."

"What's with the remote cabin anyway? Are you some sort of survivalist?"

Survivalist. That's exactly what he was. Working undercover to infiltrate a notorious drug cartel was pure survival. Never knowing when someone might turn on him or put him in an impossible situation. Constantly worried about someone discovering he was working for the FBI. Yes, his life was all about survival.

"You can say that," he mumbled.

Two years of his blood and sweat went into building this cabin. Not only secluded vacation home, but the perfect place waiting for the day when he needed to bug out. To go off-grid and hide.

He just hadn't expected it to be so soon.

Belle heaved a heavy sigh. "I'm sorry I ran from you."

"Understandable. A man assaulted you and hurled you off a cliff, then you woke here with a complete stranger."

"You're not a *complete* stranger."

He lifted his brows. "Oh, yeah?"

"Yeah," she drew out the word, examining his features. "There's something familiar…"

For a moment he held her gaze. He liked the strength behind those blue eyes. After everything she'd been through, she continued to keep her spirits up and make him smile. He wanted to know her better, learn all about her and if things were different, he'd ask her on a date. Jonah snapped his thoughts back to reality. What was he thinking? He didn't date.

He cleared his throat and moved to the window again. An idea formed and he turned. "Hey, let's start with that, the familiarity. Maybe we can get your memories to return."

"Okay," she hesitated.

"You say I look familiar. Maybe I look like someone you know from work? A family member?"

She squinted and scrutinized his face. "I don't know. I can't remember. It's something about your eyes, I think." She tensed and looked away, her shoulders rising and falling with her rapid breathing.

"Belle? What's wrong?"

"Every time I look into your eyes, I don't know." She shook her head. "This panic rises and takes over. I—I can't help it. I'm sorry."

He touched her shoulder and she flinched but didn't shrug him off. Something about her rocked him. Knocked him right off his game. He knelt in front of her and gently tipped her chin up. "Listen to me. I'm not going to hurt you. You *can* trust me."

Their gazes locked and held for a beat. "Yeah, okay." She chewed her bottom lip.

The sight of the cuts on her face and the bruising on her neck made him want to take her in his arms and protect her from the world.

She pulled her head back and fear flashed in her wide eyes.

He dropped his hand. "What? What is it?"

"Do you… Do you smell smoke?"

FOUR

Belle and Jonah jumped to their feet at the same time. The movement made her head swim, but the sensation passed quickly. She peered through the window beside Jonah. "What's going on?"

"Fire," he growled. "He set the cabin on fire."

Before she could process his words, he grabbed her hand and tugged. "C'mon."

He pulled her to the tiny kitchen area and released her hand. Squatting, he lifted the edge of the rug and threw it back. What was he doing? He crouched, giving Belle a view over his shoulder. With one hand, he dragged his fingers over the floor until they found a hidden handle of some kind. Jonah lifted, and the floor came up.

Her breath caught. A dark rectangle appeared in the floor. A secret room.

He left the door open and turned to her with his hand extended. "Let's go."

She froze. Her knees trembled and she shook her head. No. No way was she going down there. This man may have saved her life, but the sense of mistrust of what was in his eyes lingered. And what if this was a trap? A way to get her in his dark dungeon where he would...

No, she wouldn't even think about it.

"Belle, we've got to go. This cabin will go up like a matchbox. Hurry!"

Staring at the dark hole in the floor, her chest tightened, and her muscles seized. It was bad. The idea of the small space being alone with Jonah in that shadowy room made her heart palpitate. Her eyes swiveled to the front door. Could she make it? She had to try.

In one giant leap she flung herself across the room and hit the door. The heat registered for a fraction of a second before grabbing the doorknob. Flesh sizzled and she yanked her hand back. "Ow!"

Strong hands gripped her shoulders. Jonah turned her around and guided her to the hatch. He lowered himself until they were eye to eye. "Listen to me. We can't go that way. That's exactly what he wants. I have an escape room, but we have to go *now*!"

The way his dark eyes implored her caused acid to rise in her throat. Her hands trembled. "I—I can't."

"Look, I'll go first." He stepped into the hole. At his movement, a light clicked on. "See? Nothing scary. Nothing to worry about."

"No, we'll be trapped," she cried.

"We won't be trapped. It's a safe room with supplies and a hidden exit. We can get outside that way."

She wrung her shaking hands and shook her head. "No, no," she sobbed. "Please—"

A riotous crash from behind startled her. The kitchen window shattered, and flames licked at the ceiling and crept through to the walls. Black smoke rolled into the room and stung her eyes. She waved a hand and coughed.

"I know you're scared, but if you don't go with me, you'll die in this fire." His voice was calm, but firm.

She opened her mouth to protest, but he cut her off

with a hand gesture. "Belle! Listen to me. I'm an FBI agent. Come with me *now*!"

Her eyes burned. She couldn't keep them open against the blistering heat and she tasted ash. There was no choice; she had to trust him. She shuffled forward until her feet found the first step. Jonah took her hand and made room for her to go down the steps beside him.

"Hurry," he said. "I need to get this door closed."

She made it three steps down the stairs when the door slammed shut over her head. Behind her she heard the metallic clink of a bolt sliding into place, sealing them inside. Lights illuminated the rectangular white room below. Not the dingy gray dungeon she expected. It wasn't so bad. She could do this.

At the bottom of the staircase, she paused to ride out the approaching wave of nausea. Clean air filled the room and she sucked in a breath.

The vise around her head tightened until blackness crept into the corners of her eyes. No, not again. No way would she pass out down here. She drew in a breath and held it, mentally counting to ten. She released the air in a slow steady stream by blowing over pursed lips.

"Excuse me," Jonah said, scooting behind her.

He reached beneath a workbench and found a black duffel bag, dragged it out and dropped it onto the table with a heavy thump. He unzipped the bag and checked the contents.

The blackness in her periphery retreated and her head cleared. She took in the rest of her surroundings. Cans of food and plastic jugs of water filled the shelves on one side. Boxes of ammunition stacked in rows lined another shelf. Guns of assorted sizes hung on the walls and a tray table held three different pistols with several magazines laid out beside them.

"What…is…this…?" She let her words hang and ran her fingers over the hilt of a hunting knife with a long jagged blade.

He grabbed a black handled knife in a sheath and clipped it to his belt. "Survivalist, remember?"

"Yeah, I see that. Are we safe in here?"

"Not for long. This used to be an old root cellar with the cabin over it. I've modified it. Constructed it with reinforced concrete walls and a layer of fire board, so that's not the immediate problem. If he finds the hidden exit before we escape, we'll be cornered." He grabbed a pistol from the wall in front of her. "You know how to use a gun?"

She blinked. Did she? "I don't know."

"Ah, the memory loss, right." He dropped the magazine onto the table and pulled the slide back to release the bullet in the chamber.

"Here, hold this and see how it feels."

She hefted the weapon and muscle memory took over. The slide moved with ease, and she checked the chamber. Empty. With her other hand she picked up the magazine and slammed it into the bottom of the gun with a click.

"I take that as a yes. Tuck it in your waistband and only use it in an emergency."

"Thanks." She clicked the safety and tucked it at the small of her back. Somewhere in her past she had experience with firearms.

His gaze caught hers and held. "Be careful, and don't shoot the good guy, okay?"

Was he a good guy?

Every time she looked into his eyes, her pulse kicked up and a shiver ran along her spine. She should feel safe after everything he'd done, but she didn't. What kind of FBI agent looked so disheveled? With tousled hair in need of a haircut and the woolly beard he didn't look like a federal agent. Weren't they supposed to be clean-cut and wear black suits?

But then there was this safe room and his knowledge of first aid and firearms. Not many civilians had that type of training.

Well, she couldn't stay here so what choice did she have? If she wanted to get out alive, she'd have to trust Jonah. He'd protected her so far, and he seemed willing to do it again. She didn't know much about herself but knew she could fend off an attacker.

And now she had a weapon.

Jonah slipped the duffel bag onto his back and slung a larger caliber rifle across his chest. He turned to Belle. "It's time to move. Are you ready? How are you feeling?"

"I'm good," she said. "Let's get out of here while we can."

Jonah reached for her, and she hesitated before taking his hand. He gave her fingers a reassuring squeeze and tugged. "This way."

They hustled to the end of the room and into the narrow passageway he'd dug. "Watch your step right here," he said. "The floor dips. The tunnel is about fifteen yards before we reach the exit. There's no light, so be careful."

She gripped his hand tighter. "It's chilly down here."

"We're about ten feet underground. The exit is a little farther. We'll climb those stairs." He motioned to the industrial metal staircase ahead.

"Stairs? It looks like a ladder with handrails."

"Ha, well it is a steep incline, but the treads are wide. The hatch at the top leads outside. We'll come out behind my woodpile which will provide cover. We need to make it to my ATV another five yards. Think you can make it?"

"I'm fine."

The word *fine* caused him to pause. He knew that word from a woman usually meant the opposite. "We can rest a few minutes—"

"Really, Jonah, I'm fine. Adrenaline must be keeping me on my feet because I feel better."

"Okay then." He dropped her hand and placed a foot on the first step. "I'll go first but stay close. Don't come outside yet. When it's clear I'll signal you."

A fierce pop came from outside the safe room and Jonah smelled smoke. The fire would eat its way through the thick board soon.

Belle tapped his shoulder. "I've got it. Now go, before we suffocate."

Suffocation was the least of their worries, but he didn't voice his real concern. The real danger came once the fire reached his stockpile of ammunition.

He took one last look at Belle's blue eyes and hurried up the stairs. The metal hatch door creaked as he eased it open. A potentially fatal oversight. If the attacker heard the rusty hinges, it would be a dead giveaway to their location.

Jonah took a quick peek outside then ducked into the hatch. He shouldered his rifle, taking a three count to let his eyes adjust to the light. No one rushed toward the door, so he followed his weapon through the opening.

The woodpile had been strategically placed near the hatch doors as cover. He'd spent his early days of the forced sabbatical taking his frustration out by swinging an ax. The result was a cord of wood that filled the space between two trees. Perfect cover for an escape.

Belle stuck her head out the opening and watched him for a signal. He motioned for her to come out but stay low. She crawled out on her hands and knees and made it to the woodpile. Jonah helped her get to her feet. She wobbled but regained her balance.

Was this a bad idea? She'd barely made it ten steps off the porch earlier. Could she make it to the ATV? All this movement couldn't be good for her. What she needed was rest.

Jonah mouthed, *Are you okay?*

She gave him a thumbs-up and nodded.

He gestured to the area where the ATV waited. He'd stashed it in some trees under a camouflage tarp. At first glance, the four-wheeler was invisible. If the attacker stumbled upon it, he could've disabled it and they'd be in big trouble.

There was only one way to find out.

Jonah gave the signal.

Belle took off, but he didn't look. Instead, he kept his eyes on the forest and took aim at the trees beyond his pickup.

A volley of bullets pelted his barricade. Dirt and wood fragments sprayed Jonah's face, but there—he saw it. The unmistakable burst of red orange from a muzzle flash. He sighted the area through his scope. Scanned for an outline of a human. Nothing. He couldn't make out anything through the foliage. Camouflage. It had to be the same man.

A glint of metal flared to his left and he saw the bulge of a man in a supported prone position. No wonder Jonah hadn't seen him, he'd dropped to the ground. Jonah aimed and double tapped the trigger. Tree bark shattered in the distance and Jonah heard the man grunt. Jonah did a quick scan for any other threats. Seeing none, he pivoted right and bolted for his ATV.

Belle was behind the vehicle, removing the evergreen

branches he'd used to camouflage his quad and tossing them aside.

"Here, this is faster." Jonah unsheathed the small knife on his belt and cut the straps holding the tarp.

It fell and he yanked it away revealing the black-and-camouflage-painted ATV which appeared undisturbed.

"We don't have much time. I think I hit him, but I'm not sure."

Jonah supported Belle by holding her waist as she climbed onto the ATV.

"Slide forward. I'll drive from behind in case you feel faint." The ATV was built for one rider, but with Belle's small frame and his long arms, he thought he could manage.

He secured his duffel bag to the rear rack and slipped into the seat behind Belle. The engine rumbled to life on the first try and he breathed a sigh of relief. Even with Belle in front, he had plenty of room to reach the steering handles and easily see over her head.

"We're gonna move fast so hang on tight," he said. "Tap my leg if you need to stop."

"Got it—now let's get out of here."

A supersonic crack of a bullet rang out. The ground exploded in puffs of dirt and debris with each shot. A bullet tore through his shirt and nicked the flesh around his waist.

Jonah winced at the white-hot pain and hit the throttle. He steered them in the opposite direction and headed for the secret bug-out trail he'd forged. Bullets peppered the trees around them until the ATV broke through the timberline. Over his shoulder, he watched black smoke billow from the roof into the sky. Flames fully engulfed the cabin and there, standing near the woodpile, a man watched them disappear.

The bushes enveloped the ATV and provided concealment as they made their escape. Jonah leaned forward
and focused on the rutted path ahead. Decoy trails jut-
ted off in all directions. Some circled back after a mile
of twists and turns. A few meandered to nowhere. Only
Jonah knew which trails went to the right places. The
maze he'd created served as countersurveillance.

Despite his desire to stay away from the public, their
best option was Piney Village. Showing up in the rural
community was risky, but Belle needed medical attention
anyway. He was doing the right thing, even if it meant
his job and life were on the line.

He mentally mapped out the best route and settled in
for the rough drive. Belle pressed her body into his chest.
The closeness of this mysterious woman reassured him
more than he thought possible. If only he could keep
her safe.

FIVE

Belle ducked her head and lifted a hand to block a tree limb dangling over the narrow trail. The four-wheeler teetered and lurched as Jonah sped over rocks and dead limbs, putting distance between them and the attacker. The rutted trail was brutal on her sore muscles, but the headache had faded, so she wouldn't complain.

Who was the man so bent on killing her? Or…was the lunatic after Jonah? He said he was an FBI agent. Surely there was no shortage of people he'd put behind bars. Maybe this was about revenge for something in Jonah's past and had nothing to do with her.

But then why did he come after her in the woods?

No, this wasn't about Jonah. She'd brought the fight right to an innocent man's doorstep. Despite the twinge of unease that flared when she looked into his eyes, she liked the guy. He'd stepped up and put his life on the line to save her more than once today. When she broke down, he stayed cool under pressure. And what was his reward? The cabin he'd clearly worked so hard to build as an off-grid stronghold went up in flames.

Belle shifted her weight and leaned into Jonah's solid frame. His long arms wrapped around her and provided protection. It was smart to put her in front of him. Something she might not have thought about in all the chaos.

The faint smell of smoke mingled with his masculine scent, and she found it oddly comforting. Jonah was attractive, but if she'd met him on the street, she wouldn't have given him a second look.

Of course, she was no prize at the moment. Clothes covered in mud and sweat. Hair a tangled mess. And she didn't even want to think about how she smelled right now.

An image of a laboratory flashed in her mind. Aquariums filled with plants and a row of glass jars next to a microscope. The vision evaporated before she could pull details from the memory. It was a memory, wasn't it?

The pressure behind her eyes pushed out all coherent thoughts and no matter how hard she tried, she couldn't summon the image again. The headache crept back and the rumbling and vibrations of the four-wheeler weren't helping. Jonah steered the ATV around a boulder on the trail and picked up speed on the straightaway.

The rugged vehicle rolled over a massive log blocking the trail with no problem, but the impact jarred her, and she felt herself slide. Jonah's muscular arm slipped around her stomach and held her tight while he drove with his free hand.

A ripple of queasiness spread throughout her chest. Her equilibrium was off, and she had trouble keeping herself upright. Each jostle caused her to slip, forcing Jonah to hold her tighter.

She patted the firm hand grasping her middle. "Stop. I need you to stop."

Jonah tucked his chin over her shoulder and put his mouth close to her ear. "What's that?"

His hot breath on her ear sent a shiver along her neck. The way he held her tight brought one word to mind. *Safe.* She was safe with Jonah.

Unfortunately, another word popped to mind. "Dizzy. I'm feeling dizzy."

Jonah let off the throttle and the ATV came to a stop in the middle of the trail. He cut the engine and together they slipped off the vehicle.

Jonah sank to his knees with her and held her shoulders to keep her upright. "Are you okay?"

She tried to nod, but her head wouldn't cooperate. "Just…tired…"

Her muscles gave out and she collapsed into his arms. The butt of the gun in her waistband dug into her back. "Here, take this. I don't think I should handle a firearm in this condition."

"We've got to get you to a doctor." With a tender stroke, he brushed the hair from her face. "Riding over these bumps can't be good for you."

She gave him a half smile. "Maybe it will shake loose some memories."

He gave a soft laugh. "It would be nice to know your real name."

"Tell me about it," she mumbled.

He cradled her in his arms, and she examined his features. She found herself searching his face. Instead of the normal unease his eyes sparked within her, she discovered warmth and compassion. Slight stress wrinkles gathered along his forehead. It was easy to let herself relax into his embrace. The rise and fall of his firm chest with each rhythmic breath lulled her into a place of peace and she allowed her eyes to drift closed.

In this moment, her memory loss and the events of the day didn't matter. All that mattered was her sense of peace. She was *safe*.

"You know," he said in a deep voice, "I think Belle must be your name."

"Mmm hmm?"

"It must be. It's the perfect name."

She opened her eyes. "What makes you say that?"

"Didn't you know? Belle means charming. And beautiful." He stroked her cheek with the backs of his fingertips.

"Oh, yeah. Sure," she mocked. "Is it the giant bandage, or the sticks and leaves adorning my hair?"

Jonah tipped his head and laughed. He winced and touched a hand to his side.

"What's wrong?" She eased into a sitting position.

Still holding his side, he twisted and glanced at the torn fabric of his shirt. "It's nothing."

"Let me see." She touched her fingertips to his hand.

He took the hint and lifted the hem of his shirt to expose the wound on his side. "See? Nothing."

Black burn marks framed the edge of a two inch scrape in the flesh above Jonah's hip. "That's not nothing, Jonah. You've been shot!"

"Not shot. Grazed. It's not even bleeding."

He was right; the wound wasn't bleeding. It seemed to have been cauterized by the heat of the bullet. "It needs to be cleaned and covered, but it doesn't look too bad. Good thing it hit your love handles."

"Love handles!" Jonah laughed. "I don't have love handles!"

"Riiiiight." She gave him an exaggerated eye roll that made her head spin. Better not do that again for a while.

Jonah smiled. "You know, you sure are a hoot."

"A *hoot*? No one says hoot anymore unless they're an owl. I think you've been living the hermit life a bit too long."

"Maybe, or maybe it's just been too long since I've had a good laugh." His smile faded and she sensed sadness behind his words.

"Can you tell me about it?"

"I wish I could," he sighed. "It's an ongoing investigation."

"Right. Of course. I'm sure an FBI agent needs to be discreet."

He gave her a curt nod and studied her. Was he looking at her messy hair? She made a futile attempt to tame it with a hand. Nothing but a long shower could help her now.

She cleared her still sore throat. "Did you bring a first aid kit?"

"Let me grab it." Jonah unfolded his long legs and stood. He rummaged around in the duffel bag on the ATV and set a red box with a white cross on the seat.

"I'll do it," she said as she stood and dusted the dirt off her hands.

"You should rest—I can take care of it."

"Don't be such a man about it. Got any gloves?"

He grinned and handed her a pair.

In less than a minute she'd slathered antibiotic cream over the wound and covered it with gauze, taking extra care to tape off the edges to keep debris out.

"There. That should do for now. Now we'll both need to see the doctor when we get to town." She lowered his shirt to cover the bandage and pulled the gloves off. "Time to get moving again?"

Jonah tucked the trash and the kit into his bag and pulled out two bottles of water. "Rest a few minutes longer. We're several miles from the cabin, so we'll be all right for a while."

His cabin. Somewhere behind them, Jonah's home burned. All his belongings, all his arduous work. Gone. "I'm sorry about your cabin, Jonah."

"Yeah, me too." A shadow passed over his face. "It's

not important right now. What's important is we escaped before—"

A crack of gunfire cut his words.

Jonah's ears heard the shot before it fully registered. Instinctively, he grabbed Belle and pulled her down, using the ATV as cover. How did the gunman find them so fast?

Dozens of bullets exploded and Jonah recognized the distant staccato sound as the ammunition in his cabin discharging as the bullet casings melted in the fire.

"It's okay," he said, pulling Belle to her feet. "It's not a shooter. The ammunition in my bunker is letting off. We need to find a spot and call the ranger station."

"Wow, that sounds dangerous. We need to tell someone before they step foot near the cabin." She looked up. "I see a bit of sky overhead. Maybe try for a signal now."

Jonah found the phone in his bag and powered it on. The call wouldn't connect. "I can't get a signal with all the clouds and trees. I need an open sky."

"So, let's get to an opening. Why waste any more time here?" She drained her water bottle and handed him the empty container.

It seemed vital to tell law enforcement about their situation. The recent rains should contain the fire for a while, but Belle was right, they should be warned about the ammunition.

He crushed the bottle and put it in the bag, then dropped the phone into his pocket. "Going out in the open for a signal is risky. Whoever shot at us and set my cabin on fire could see us, so we need to be careful."

"Yes, but if we don't take the risk, other lives could be in jeopardy." She climbed onto the ATV. "This time I'll sit behind you, so I have something to hold on to."

"Are you sure?"

"Yeah, I think the water helped."

He mounted the four-wheeler in front of Belle and cranked the engine. It roared to life. Belle slid her arms around his waist and brushed against the bandaged bullet graze. A zing of pain raced through his side, and he bit his lower lip to silence himself. He didn't want Belle to think she'd hurt him. After all she'd been through, his injury wasn't worth another thought.

"If you need to stop, pat my chest to get my attention," he said.

She gave him three hardy thwacks. "Got it. Let's roll."

Jonah grinned. He found himself enjoying Belle's company and her quirky sense of humor. They'd only met a few hours ago, yet her playful teasing and bright spirit made it seem like they'd known each other for years. A joy and happiness radiated from her even after all she'd been through today, and the warmth of her smile drew him in.

He took the trail a bit slower now. Careful to avoid the biggest rocks that would rattle Belle. The trail snaked around trees and boulders as they climbed in elevation. An opening in the path ahead indicated a crossroads he recognized. He let off the throttle and rolled to a stop before he reached the intersection.

Clouds hung low in the sky, but the canopy of trees thinned. Maybe this would work. He pulled the phone from his pocket and saw the signal indicator had a single bar. "Looks like I can make a call, but I don't want to stop for long. You good?"

"Yes, but I'm eager to get to Piney Village." Her hands covered her stomach. "I'm *starving*."

Hunger hadn't occurred to Jonah. With his job, he often went all day without eating. In his undercover work, he was up all hours of the night building relationships with members of a drug cartel. His days were spent in debriefing meetings followed by hours of paperwork. Most of his meals consisted of coffee and whatever he found in the break room.

Good thing he kept snacks handy for long days out on the trail. "Check the utility box on your right."

Belle unlatched the lid and peeked inside. Her face lit up when she saw his snack stash. "Oh! Bless you!" She tore into a bag of trail mix and closed her eyes while she chewed the first handful.

"Take as much as you want. There's beef jerky in there somewhere and bottles of water. Just don't eat too fast or it might make you sick."

"At least I'll have something in my stomach to throw up." She gave a mock shiver. "Those dry heaves are a killer."

Jonah shook his head at her and smiled. "After I make the call, we'll get to town and find you some real food."

He dismounted the ATV and scrolled the contacts on his phone until he found the number for the ranger station. To his surprise, it connected right away.

"Ranger station." The man answered with a weathered voice.

"Yes, I'd like to report a cabin fire—"

"Name?"

"Jonah. We—"

"Is the fire contained?"

"I think so."

"Is everyone out of the home?"

"Yes, and—"

The ranger interrupted again. "Address of the home?"

With a pang of regret at losing the privacy of his bug-out cabin, Jonah rattled off the address. "Listen, there's more. The fire was arson. A stranger set fire to my cabin and fired a gun at us, but we managed to escape."

"We?"

"I have a woman with me." He slid his eyes to Belle who was biting off a hunk of jerky and watching him. "I think the same man tried to attack her by Eagle Lake."

Belle stopped chewing midbite.

"Can you describe the attacker?"

This was taking too long. He wanted to report the fire and get moving, not tell his life story to the man. "I'm reporting the fire, but we escaped on my ATV about half an hour ago. I have no idea how involved the fire is by now, but I heard my stock of ammunition discharging, so approach with caution. I'm heading to Piney Village to report the incident to the sheriff."

The ranger was quiet, but Jonah could hear the click of a keyboard in the background. "We'll get someone to check out the fire and the attacker, but I must warn you, it could take a while. The search and rescue team has been locating a group of missing hikers, and whoever wasn't on the search team is working injuries from the landslide. With all the rain, the fire shouldn't spread and since this isn't a life-or-death situation, we need to focus our attention on the landslide. Sheriff Riley should be in his office in the next hour."

"I understand," Jonah said. The ranger was saying Jonah's cabin would be a total loss by the time someone put the fire out. "Have all the missing hikers been found?"

"Yes, all are accounted for."

Jonah eyed Belle. If she wasn't one of the hikers, why hadn't anyone reported her missing? He'd have to ask the sheriff later. For now, they needed to keep moving.

"Thanks, we'll check in with Sheriff Riley and let him take things from here. You can reach me at this number."

"I'll contact the sheriff and let him know to expect you," he said. "More rain is expected overnight. Watch for flash floods and falling rocks."

That's not all they'd be on the lookout for. He looked to the forest beyond the trail.

The gunman was still somewhere out there, and Jonah's gut told him this guy wouldn't stop until he found Belle.

SIX

The first glimpse of Piney Village caused Belle to suck in a breath. White-capped mountains surrounded the town and reflected off the shimmering lake in the center. Modest log cabins lined a small section of the shore with yellow wildflowers covering a field spanning to the base of the mountain. A fast-moving stream stretched from the edge of the lake and meandered off into the distance.

Belle eyed the area of the lake closest to the mountain. A thin green film of algae grew along the top of the water. Curiosity nudged her memory. Was it the lake? The algae? She couldn't put her finger on it but stared at the green film until they'd driven out of view.

Jonah drove the ATV over a single-lane bridge with rust-red metal guardrails and a wood deck that spanned a rocky stream. The clear water hurried over smooth rocks and boulders in a rush to get down the mountain. Mesmerized by the picturesque scene and burbling water, Belle jolted when the ATV left the bridge.

The gravel road in front of the cabins forked and Jonah steered onto a paved road leading to the village. The entire town appeared to consist of this one paved road called Main Street. Three blocks of nineteenth-century historical buildings lined each side of the road. Most were two-story brick with colorful awnings over the windows. Old barrel planters filled with vibrant flowers dotted the sidewalks, and benches offered a place to sit on each block. Each building appeared to be historically preserved. Belle found the village enchanting.

They rode past an ancient bank, a hardware store and a small diner. Pedestrians strolled on the sidewalk but didn't give them a second glance. Probably used to off-road vehicles in town.

The sheriff's office was the last building on the corner. A white brick building that she almost mistook for a storefront. A gold sheriff's star on each window the only indication they'd found the right place. Had Belle not watched closely they might have missed it.

He parked the ATV on the street behind a silver pickup truck and went inside. A bored-looking woman sat in front of a computer, twirling a lock of her shoulder-length black hair and reading a paperback novel. Her nameplate identified her as Annie Reed.

Annie looked up and grinned. "Oh, hi there!" She flipped her book over and dropped the twisted hair. Her voice cheerful and pleasant. "How can I help you?"

Jonah stepped nearer and smiled. "Afternoon. Is the sheriff in?"

"Oh, no he's not actually. I'm so sorry. He's over at Stella's place. Not sure when he'll be back exactly."

"Stella?"

"Oh, you're not from around here, are you?" She smacked her forehead with her palm. "Dr. Stella Park. Sheriff's there having her look at a cut— Oh, she's not a medical doctor, she's a vet. I mean a veterinarian. But she does pass for a doctor around here. We don't have a town doctor anymore after, well never mind. I can call ahead, but you should get going so Stella can take a look at your injury." She paused to nod at Belle.

Belle couldn't help smiling at Annie. The rapid-fire babbling was perhaps a symptom of so few visitors in the small town. The poor girl probably hadn't talked to anyone for hours.

"Where can we find Stella Park?" Jonah asked.

Annie giggled. "I don't s'pose you'd know that, now would ya? Some days I think I'd lose my own head if it weren't attached."

She reached for a pen and quickly sketched out a map. "Basically, you'll head back the way you came and go past Piney Lake, over the bridge. Did you come over the bridge? It's new. Just put in last year. Keep going until you see the sign for Park Animal Clinic right here." She tapped the spot on her map with her index finger. "It's her house, but also the clinic. Go right in the front door."

Annie gave them the directions and an open invitation for dinner any night. They thanked her and left. Jonah helped Belle climb onto the ATV and she scooted to make room for him.

"She sure was friendly," said Jonah.

"I think she was flirting with you," she teased.

Jonah balked and started the engine. It wouldn't surprise Belle if Annie was flirting with Jonah. He was the epitome of tall, dark and handsome and probably the only single man this side of the Rio Grande.

He was single, wasn't he?

Belle never asked. But there wasn't a single feminine thing about his cabin, and she hadn't noticed a wedding ring. Maybe he didn't wear one. She decided to let it go for now and leaned into his back as he pulled away from the curb.

They retraced their path over the gravel road to the Park Animal Clinic. Belle almost sighed when the ATV hit the smooth blacktop driveway leading to the house.

The constant vibration and bouncing over the craggy road only increased the pain throbbing in her head.

From the driveway, the animal clinic was a welcoming two-story home on a sprawling ranch. The horse barn matched the appearance of the house with the exception of a rail fence enclosing a paddock on one side. Both structures had cedar doors, a lean-to porch, plank siding and a metal roof. Jonah followed the driveway to the house and parked beside a silver SUV with the sheriff's logo on the door.

"Wow, this place is gorgeous," Belle said.

The covered veranda spanned the front of the home with a group of rocking chairs on one end and a hanging bench on the other. Belle found the home charming and she could picture herself cuddled with a book, enjoying the tranquility. She eyed the evenly spaced planters and sensed she knew the names of the plants but couldn't pull the words from her memory.

A tiny sign invited them to Come On In.

She looked at Jonah and he held the screen door open for her. "After you."

They stepped into a waiting room with a reception counter on the left. A dark brown German shorthaired pointer stretched and trotted over.

"Well, hello there. Aren't you a beauty?" Belle extended the back of her hand and let the dog sniff. He nudged her with his cold nose, and she ran her hands over his sleek coat. "Nice to meet you too."

"That's Oscar," said a woman's voice.

Belle glanced up to see a tall woman striding down the hallway toward them. Her long blond hair was pulled into a ponytail that accentuated high cheekbones and a sharp nose. She wore muddy hiking boots, faded jeans and a red flannel shirt over a white tank top.

"And I'm Stella Park." She greeted them with a handshake and a wide sunny smile that made her hazel eyes sparkle. "Excuse our appearance. Oscar and I just returned from locating a group of hikers caught in the landslide."

"Oscar is a rescue dog?" Belle asked.

"Well, yes and no. He's certified in wilderness tracking, which means he needs a starting point and a scent to follow. In this case, the hikers left their campsite for a short day hike so we tracked them from there."

"Wow, he's been a busy boy today," Jonah said, patting Oscar.

"Yes, he has. Which is why he needs his rest," Stella said. "Okay, Oscar, bed."

The dog hung his head and padded to the oversize dog bed nestled in the corner.

"Don't look at me like that," Stella said to Oscar. She eyed Belle's bandaged forehead. "I'm sure you didn't come here for an education on working dogs. What happened?"

"I'm sorry. We didn't introduce ourselves. My name is Jonah, and this is Belle. We came to talk to Sheriff Riley and get medical attention if possible."

Stella surveyed Belle's head injury. "Sure, but I'm not a medical doctor, I'm a veterinarian. Piney Village hasn't had a physician for a while so I've stepped in where I can. I'm a trained paramedic, though. Thought I wanted to be a trauma surgeon before I switched to vet school. Minor medical emergencies and treatment are no problem, as long as you understand."

"We heard the landslide covered the only road down the mountain and there's no hope for a hospital unless it's life-or-death, so it sounds like you're our best option," Belle said.

Stella nodded. "They're working on clearing the debris, but it will be a few days yet. They always start with the highways and work their way up the mountain to the little guys. LifeLine choppers are on standby for critical patients, of course. But you're walking and talking so I doubt you'd qualify. Follow me and let's take a look."

She headed down the hallway, talking over her shoulder. "Linc…I mean Sheriff Riley is here but stepped outside for a call. I'll let him know you'd like to speak to him."

The exam room looked familiar, but then weren't all exam rooms the same? Counter, sink, chairs, jars of cotton swabs. The one thing Belle didn't expect was a padded examination table.

She climbed onto the paper-lined surface. "Wow, you offer your patients real comfort."

Stella grinned and flopped onto a rolling stool. "This room is reserved for my *human* patients," she said. She plucked gloves from a box and pulled them on. "The majority of my patients are livestock and I treat them in the barn out back. I have other rooms for small animals."

There was a soft knock and Stella rolled herself to the door. She smiled when she saw the uniformed officer. "Hey, Linc. You're just the man this couple wanted to see."

Belle started to correct her. They weren't a *couple*. They were…wait, what were they? Strangers really. Two people thrown together by circumstance. No point in explaining it right now, so she let the remark hang.

The barrel-chested officer dipped his bald head in greeting. He had soft brown eyes and a clean shave from his square jaw to his tanned scalp. "Howdy, folks. I'm Sheriff Lincoln Riley. You the couple who called the ranger about your cabin?"

"Yes, sir," Jonah said, extending a hand. "Jonah Phillips."

The sheriff waved his bandaged right hand at Jonah. "Rain check on that handshake. Nasty cut earlier. Doc stitched me up."

"You better take care of that too," Stella warned. "I was about to examine Belle. Do you mind?"

Riley raised his hands in mock surrender. "Oh, I beg your pardon."

"If Belle doesn't mind, I'd like you to stay," Jonah said. "Get her statement while it's fresh."

"Fine with me," Belle said. She was exhausted and wanted to get this over with so she could find food and a place to sleep for about three weeks straight.

Riley closed the door and pulled a pencil and notebook from his breast pocket. "Statement, huh?"

Stella patted Belle's leg with a gloved hand. "Okay, so tell us what happened."

Belle shifted her gaze to Jonah. He leaned against the wall with his arms folded and nodded for her to take the lead. She looked at her hands, suddenly aware of the dirt and soot caked under her nails and in the lines of her knuckles.

With a heavy sigh she said, "Well… That's part of the problem. I… I don't remember."

Jonah's gut clenched at Belle's admission of memory loss. Despite how much they'd been through, he was reminded how little he really knew about the woman. Sitting on the exam table with her head low and fidgeting with her hands, she looked small and vulnerable.

Maybe this was a mistake. How could a veterinarian treat a head injury with amnesia? Cuts and bruises sure, but an injury like Belle's required a specialist. An MRI and neurological testing in a real hospital. But what choice did they have? He should've taken her to the diner to eat, then found a place where she could rest while he called his handler. Chase needed to know what happened, but Jonah couldn't very well call him right now. It would have to wait until he was alone, so no one overheard their conversation.

Stella cocked an eyebrow and glanced between Jonah and Belle. "Are you saying you have total memory loss?"

"Kinda. I was attacked in the woods—I remember that," Belle said. "But I can't remember who attacked me, or why."

"Amnesia?" Sheriff Riley asked.

Belle shrugged. "I guess."

"Okay, let's start with your name," Riley said. He checked his notebook. "Jonah Phillips and…"

"I don't know my real name," Belle mumbled.

"If you don't remember your name, then why did he call you Belle? Don't you two know each other?" Riley darted his gaze between Belle and Jonah.

Jonah drew his hand over his face. This was his fault. Starting the interview in the exam room was a bad idea. He thought having Belle explain her injuries to Sheriff Riley and Dr. Park at the same time would make it easier on her. Clearly it only caused Belle frustration when she needed to stay calm.

"Listen, I'm not so sure we should continue until after Dr. Park—"

"Stella. Just Stella," she said.

Jonah nodded. "I'm concerned we're making things worse for Belle. Shouldn't she be resting? I can stop by the sheriff's office and give you a formal statement after doctor—I mean Stella, finishes."

"How about the sheriff holds his questions while I start my examination. Jonah, you can tell us what happened,

and Belle can chime in when she feels like it. Mmm?"
Stella squeezed Belle's shoulder.

"Works for me," Riley said.

Jonah recounted the events of the day including how
the attacker pushed Belle over the bluff and she hit her
head. "Before she lost consciousness, I asked her name
and she mumbled something that sounded like Belle."

"Since I can't remember my real name, we're going
with it for now," Belle said. "Do you think the memory
loss is permanent?"

Stella clipped a pulse oximeter to Belle's index finger. "I'm sorry, but there is no way to know right now.
You'll need a brain scan and psychological tests. How
'bout you tell me what happened when you regained consciousness."

"I woke up in Jonah's cabin and...well," Belle's voice
dipped to an almost whisper. "I guess I was confused
and thought he was my attacker and he'd kidnapped me."

"I can't blame you for that," Jonah said. "You were
disoriented."

Belle gave him a half smile. "I'm *still* disoriented."
She sucked air between her teeth as Stella pulled the
bandage from her temple.

"Sorry, got a bit of hair. This cut isn't bad, but it needs a
few stitches," Stella said. "I can do it right now as long as
you understand normally I only stitch creatures with fur."

Riley waved his bandaged hand. "Don't let her fool
you. She's very skilled."

"Yeah, okay. It's fine with me," Belle said.

Stella began the process of suturing Belle's wound
and Riley aimed his questions toward Jonah. "Can you
describe the assailant?"

Jonah exhaled. "Every time I got a look at the guy, he
was dressed in hunting camouflage and too far away to

get a good look at his face. I'd say Caucasian, about my height, six-three, black hair, somewhere between late twenties to late thirties. Belle had a closer look."

"I'd agree with Jonah's description. He wore a baseball hat, but I knocked it off. His eyes were dark, almost black. I know him, or at least I think I do, but I can't quite put my finger on it."

Riley looked Jonah over. Probably thinking Jonah fit the description of the attacker. "That's all right. It'll come to you. Keep going."

Jonah told Riley about the shooting near his truck and the fire at the cabin. "We escaped through my old root cellar, and he began shooting at us, so I returned fire. We made it to my ATV and came here."

"Did you hit him?" Riley asked.

"Not sure. I heard him grunt, so it's possible. But I can tell you this much, either he didn't really want to hit us, or he is a terrible shot."

"Not too terrible," Belle piped in. "He got you in the side."

Stella paused and looked over her shoulder. "What? Why didn't you say something?"

"It's just a graze, nothing serious. Take a look when you're finished there."

She frowned and turned to Belle. She applied a clean bandage over the stitches. "Keep this covered for the next two days and try not to bump it. You can take a shower but keep the area dry for a week. You'll need to have these removed in three to five days."

"Thank you so much," Belle said.

After a thorough examination and a few more questions, Stella diagnosed Belle with a mild to moderate concussion. "It's not urgent, but as soon as the road is cleared, you should go to the hospital for further tests. The nausea and dizziness should subside in a day or two."

"What about my memory?"

"In most cases, memories return on their own over time. The best thing is to rest. Keep the stress to a minimum."

"Any idea when the road will be clear?" Jonah asked.

Riley sighed. "It could take a day or two. The landslide covered some heavily trafficked roads, and my guess is we're last on the list."

"Well, that could be an issue," Jonah said. "My cabin burned down, and I didn't see any motels when we drove through town. We're kinda homeless."

"And hungry," Belle said.

"That's not a problem," Stella said. "You'll stay here as long as you need. I've got three extra bedrooms besides the apartment out in the barn where my ranch hand lives with his wife. And having you close means I can keep an eye on Belle in case her condition changes. As for the hunger, I was about to make dinner, so you're just in time to eat."

"Are you sure it's safe to stay here?" Belle asked. "What about the attacker? He could—"

"You let me worry about that," Stella said.

Riley closed his notebook. "I think that's a great idea. I'll have my deputy patrol the area and keep an eye out. Besides, I might have more questions for you, and I'll know right where to find you."

"Thank you both so much," Belle said.

"I'm going to investigate this," Riley said waving his notebook. "There've been a few incidents recently. Other attacks that could be connected. I may need you to come to the station, but I'll let you know. Here's my card. Call if you need anything."

Jonah took the sheriff's card and tucked it in his back

pocket. "Thanks, Sheriff. We'll check in with you tomorrow and see if there's any update."

Stella nodded at Riley as he left, then turned serious. "Okay, now let me see this gunshot wound."

SEVEN

Strange dreams kept Belle tossing and turning throughout the night. But were they dreams, or hidden memories trying to resurface? She wasn't sure. She stared at the ceiling and tried to recall her name. Her address. Her job. The type of car she drove.

Nothing.

Think, brain. Think.

The covers pressed on her and became suffocating. She kicked her feet free and rolled out of bed. The tangled mess of blankets and sheets wadded up on the bed irked her. Was she the type of person who couldn't stand an unmade bed? She yanked the covers toward her and found the edges. Flicked them to shake out the wrinkles. They drifted down and landed flat on the bed. A pillow rested on the floor near her feet, so she picked it up and punched it a few times before arranging it against the headboard.

With her hands on her hips, she surveyed her work. There. That was better.

A pink Bible rested on the nightstand, and she reached for it. Ran her thumb over the cover. This…this was familiar.

She hopped onto the bed and opened the Bible. Her eyes fell to a scripture. "'The LORD *is* good, a strong hold in the day of trouble,'" she read out loud, "'and he knoweth them that trust in him.'"

"He sure does."

Belle noticed Stella standing in the doorway. "Come in," she said.

"Sorry to interrupt. The door was cracked so I thought I'd peek in on you. How do you feel today?"

"Better, I think." She closed the Bible and pushed it away. "I haven't puked today, so there's that."

Stella laughed. "Well, that's something. What about your head? Are you dizzy? Nauseous?"

"Actually, no. I have a slight headache, but I think it's caffeine withdrawal. I really need coffee."

"Okay!" Stella clapped her hands and smiled brightly. "Let's get you some coffee!"

Stella was far more enthusiastic about coffee than Belle would have guessed. Of course, some people were total addicts just like…like…*her.*

"Hey! I like coffee!" She jumped to her feet. "No, I *love* coffee! I remember!"

Belle couldn't help herself. She rushed to Stella and wrapped her arms around the woman. They hugged for a few moments and Belle said a silent prayer of thanks to God.

"You had a memory!" Stella pulled back and held Belle by the arms. "I think it deserves coffee *and* breakfast."

"Knock, knock." Jonah stuck his head in the open doorway. "Did I hear something about breakfast?"

Belle stepped back from Stella. "Oh, hey. Good morning. Yeah, I was just about to change and come down."

Butterflies danced in her stomach at the sight of Jonah freshly showered and changed. The thick beard covering most of his face was trimmed close. She wanted to tell him he looked good but realized her own appearance was less than desirable.

Stella lifted an eyebrow at Belle knowingly. "Morning, Jonah. What do you say we start the coffee and give Belle time to freshen up?" She headed toward the door but paused. "I left some clean clothes and toiletries in the bathroom for you. Take your time."

"Thanks, I don't know what we'd do without you."

Stella and Jonah headed downstairs chattering about coffee and western omelets.

Belle loved how Stella built her house with a clinic connected but separate from the main house. Over dinner last night, Stella explained how the barn behind the house contained the main area of her veterinarian clinic and another barn housed her horses and livestock.

The house itself had three bedrooms upstairs, each with a private bath. Downstairs was a primary suite, a small office and the open living room, kitchen and dining room. She wouldn't tell Jonah, but Belle preferred Stella's place to his rustic cabin with the outhouse. Of course, it was probably the only part of Jonah's house still standing. A shiver ran along her spine at the thought of that outhouse.

When Belle saw herself in the mirror she gasped. A dark blue bruise surrounded the bandage on her temple. The purple under her eyes was probably stress related, but the bruises on her neck…wow. She tipped her head to the side and examined the bluish-purple lines stretching from the back of her neck to beneath her chin. Her attacker's finger impressions.

She grabbed the ends of her hair and pulled them forward in an attempt to cover the marks. It didn't work. Her hair bounced back. Stella had helped her wash her hair last night but sleeping on wet hair caused her curls to frizz into a puffy red helmet. Perfect. She wouldn't be able to tame her hair beast without her special hair products.

Hair products! It was a tiny detail from her everyday life, but she was elated to know she used something to tame her curls. But what was the name? Something curl keeper? Why couldn't she remember? She braced herself on the edge of the counter, gripping it until her knuckles turned white.

The Bible verse she read earlier came to mind.

The LORD is *good, a strong hold in the day of trouble; and he knoweth them that trust in him.*

Yes, that was it! The memories came when she least expected them. She couldn't explain it but knew deep down she could trust God. And if she didn't force it, her memories would come back on their own.

She dressed in the clothes Stella had left and did her best with her hair. After she brushed her teeth twice for good measure, she headed for the kitchen. The smell of coffee met her halfway down the stairs and she smiled knowing she needed that morning caffeine boost. With a little milk and sugar of course.

Jonah stood and pulled a chair out for her. "How are you feeling?"

"Amazing considering the circumstances. Did Stella tell you I like coffee?" She took the offered seat and poured herself a cup from the carafe.

Stella placed a platter of omelets and a bowl of biscuits in the center of the table. "She remembered she likes coffee, but then again, who doesn't?"

"But that's not all—I remembered I use hair products to subdue this wild mess." She gestured to her hair. "And, I know God."

"Know God? What does that mean?" Jonah asked.

She took a sip of her coffee and let her shoulders rise and fall in appreciation. "Mmm, delicious." She took another sip then looked at Jonah. "I'm a Christian."

"Oh." Jonah averted his eyes. "Should we eat? Or do we need to *pray* first?"

The edge in his voice didn't escape Belle's notice. Was he offended by her comment? She had no idea how to respond so she didn't.

"Good idea. I'll bless the food," Stella said. "God, thank You for our new friendship even under these circumstances. Heal Jonah and Belle quickly and flood Belle's memories back. Bless this food. Amen."

"Amen," Belle echoed. During the prayer, Belle silently asked God to give her more memories today. Any memories. She'd even take some bad ones at this point.

They made their plates and ate in quiet. Starving, Belle had to force herself to slow and chew her food before swallowing. Last night she went to bed with her belly full of venison stew with potatoes, carrots and hunks of elk meat. This morning she was famished again, and Stella knew how to cook.

"So, Jonah," Stella said, "what do you do for a living?"

Jonah's mouth was filled with a bite of biscuit, and he held up a finger suggesting he couldn't answer until he swallowed.

Belle waited, but Jonah continued to chew so she answered for him, "He's an FBI agent."

Jonah's breath caught at Belle's announcement, and he coughed, spewing bits of biscuit. His body took over and tried to suck air into his lungs and swallow at the same time.

Wrong move.

Biscuit crumbs made their way into his windpipe and

sent him into a spasm of coughs. Hand over his mouth, he slid his chair back and hurried to the kitchen sink. The wound on his side burned with each cough, but it would have to take a backseat to his current not breathing issue. He leaned his head over the sink and let himself cough.

Stella was beside him. "Don't panic. Try to clear your throat by saying, *ahem* with as much force as you can."

Belle stood beside Stella and placed a hand on his back.

An audience. How awesome.

Tears formed in his eyes as if the liquid could somehow expel the biscuit, but he did as Stella suggested. One big throat clear and a mushy hunk of bread dislodged. Even with his airway clear he continued to cough, but with less ferocity.

"Are you okay now?" Belle asked.

Jonah rubbed his face and nodded.

He turned and leaned against the counter. Orange juice pooled on the table and dribbled to the floor. In his rush to get to the sink, he must've knocked his glass over.

Stella grabbed a roll of paper towels. "I'll clean up the juice, so no one slips."

"Here." Belle offered a cup of water.

The cool liquid soothed his throat and he forced himself to sip rather than gulp. She ran a comforting hand over his shoulder, and he wanted to kick himself for being the one in need. It was only a few seconds but being unable to breathe challenged his unflappable nature. He prided himself in the ability to keep calm in all situations but being starved for air…that was too much.

He studied the bruises around Belle's neck and his blood ran hot. That man had pressed his fingers into Belle's throat and cut off her air supply. Squeezed until she couldn't breathe. He'd just experienced an ounce of what she went through, and it was terrifying.

He put the cup in the sink and gave Belle a side hug. "Thanks." He coughed and wiped his eyes with the back of his hand. "Went down the wrong pipe."

"Clearly," Belle deadpanned.

Despite his aching throat, he tried to laugh but it sounded more like a wheeze. For a moment, he thought he might have another coughing fit, but it passed. "Wow, I think I need some fresh air."

"Why don't you head outside, and I'll help Stella with the cleaning," Belle said.

"I can help—"

Belle placed a hand on his forearm. "It's okay—we can handle this. Go on and I'll join you with a fresh cup of coffee in a few minutes."

Outside, Jonah gripped the porch railing and breathed in the fresh air. It had rained most of the night, but it was a clear summer morning. Hemmed in by white-capped mountains with the lake in the center, he could see why the people of Piney Village chose to live in this remote place. The crisp air and sounds of nature offered peace and clarity. Something he desperately needed after Belle's announcement.

The phone in his pocket vibrated and Jonah saw it was Chase Bishop, the assistant special agent in charge who served as Jonah's contact while undercover.

Jonah moved to sit on the porch swing and accepted the call. "Were your ears burning?"

"Talking me up again? Hopefully it's to a beautiful woman—on the right side of the law this time." Chase laughed.

"Well…that's the thing," Jonah said.

"Wait. I wasn't being serious."

Jonah recounted the entire story of finding Belle and the attacker shooting at them then burning down his cabin forcing them to flee. "With the landslide covering the roads, we can't get off the mountain so we're staying at Dr. Stella Park's house in Piney Village."

Chase groaned. "You're supposed to be laying low, remember? I need you completely off-grid, so no one recognizes you and runs to the news."

"Yeah well, tell that to the guy who set my house on fire." Jonah stood and paced the length of the porch. "Besides. Piney Village is about as off-grid as a town can be. And what was I supposed to do? Let the woman lie there and drown?"

"No, of course not. According to the wiretaps we have in place, it sounds like your cover is still intact. They think you got picked up on a minor drug possession and you're waiting it out in the county jail."

Jonah scratched his beard. It itched and he couldn't wait to shave it off completely, but for now it was the mask he wore to protect his identity.

"You think Belle's attacker is the Trailside Strangler?" Jonah asked. "I mean, he's never used a gun that we know of. And he's never hunted around here, but we know it's his dumping ground. Maybe Belle was in the wrong place at the wrong time and he couldn't help himself."

Chase was quiet for several seconds, but Jonah could hear the clicking of a pen on the other end of the phone. An annoying habit that drove Jonah up the wall when he was on desk duty.

"It's possible the killer stumbled on your mystery woman, but it seems too coincidental. I'll run it by the profiler and get back to you. For now, I think we need to bring the sheriff into the loop. We don't want him uncovering your identity and compromising the case."

"Yeah, I'd rather avoid that circus," Jonah said.

"Good, I'll call him right away. Want us to pull you in? Put you up in a safe house?"

Jonah turned and saw Belle on the other side of the screen door, a cup of coffee in each hand. He held the door for her and indicated his phone. She flashed him a grin and put his coffee on the rail before curling up on the porch swing with her own mug. Feet tucked underneath, she stared toward the mountains. Warmth spread through Jonah's chest, and he couldn't take his eyes off her.

He cleared his throat. "I, um. I think I can stay here a while longer. Might be good to keep an eye on Belle."

It was risky staying in a town rather than holed up in a safe house, but the last time he'd put his career first, he'd lost the woman he'd thought he'd marry. The pen clicking paused and Jonah heard keyboard taps. "Piney Village you said?"

"Yep."

"The town is small enough. I think you can lay low there a few days."

"Will do. I need to go for now."

"One more thing," Chase said. "The analysts on the Trailside Strangler case had a few questions about your SF-86. You know, the national security questionnaire you completed before attending Quantico?"

"Yeah? What about it?" He waited, but Chase didn't continue. Jonah let the silence stretch.

If Chase was expecting Jonah to confess some deep dark secret, he'd be disappointed. Jonah was an open book. The FBI knew everything about his life right down to the cover story he used to infiltrate the drug cartel. Raised in a loving Christian home, his childhood was idyllic. That was, until his mom was diagnosed with breast cancer and his dad died in the line of duty during her treatment.

Enough guessing. He wanted facts.

"Was there something you wanted to say?"

"Well, I'm wondering why you didn't disclose a pretty major detail about your birth."

"My what? I don't think I'm following."

Chase exhaled into the phone and clicked his pen twice. "By the sound of your voice, I'm guessing no one ever told you that you were adopted."

EIGHT

Belle watched the color drain from Jonah's face. The person on the other end of the phone call dropped a bombshell, and the devastation took shape in Jonah's body language.

"That is information I didn't have. Let me get back to you on that." He disconnected the call and carried his coffee to the porch swing. "May I?" He gestured to the spot next to her.

"Of course." She unfolded a leg and let it dangle. When he was settled beside her, she ventured a guess at the call. "Bad news?"

Jonah slurped his coffee and stretched his long legs outward. With a slight bend in his knee, he pushed them in a gentle swing. "More like...unexpected news. My ASAC—"

"ASAC?"

"Oh, that stands for assistant special agent in charge of my field office. I said I'd like to stay with you a while longer, and he's agreed."

"I see." Belle stared into her coffee. "You know, Jonah, I don't need you to babysit me."

"Oh, that's not...I mean, that wasn't the unexpected news. That's good news, in fact." He nudged her with his elbow. "I *get* to stay here with you."

She couldn't suppress the smile that crept onto her lips. A spark ignited deep inside, and her heart thudded at the thought of spending more time near Jonah. How could she have thought he wanted to hurt her? All he'd ever done was help her and take care of her as best he could. Even now. Because her own legs were too short to reach the porch, he rocked the swing at the perfect rhythm that wouldn't spill their coffee.

Energy coursed through her body and searched for an exit. She had to move. "Think it's safe enough to go for a walk?"

"I think so. Besides, I could use the fresh air." He put their cups on the porch rail and held the swing so she could hop down. "Let's take our coffee inside and let Stella know. I'll grab my sidearm to be safe."

Inside, Belle washed the mugs in the kitchen sink while Jonah went to find Stella. After she dried the cups, she slipped onto a stool at the counter to wait. She could hear Jonah and Stella's faint voices from upstairs.

Belle touched the bandage at her temple, surprised it wasn't more painful. Her entire body was stiff and sore, but a walk would help to loosen her muscles. She was glad Stella had found comfortable clothes and tennis shoes she could wear, even if the shoes were a half size too big.

A few minutes later, Jonah trotted down the stairs with a jacket in his hand. "I thought you might need this. Stella says there's a trail that winds around Piney Lake and I figured it might get chilly."

"Thanks, that's incredibly thoughtful," she said. He held the jacket out so she could slip it on.

They headed outside and followed the worn trail leading away from Stella's ranch. They walked in quiet for a while. Listening to the sounds of their footsteps on the dirt path. Jonah intentionally shortened his strides to keep pace with her. His watchfulness didn't escape her notice either. Head up, he studied their surroundings. Knowing he would keep her safe eased her mind.

The scenery was breathtaking, and a thought pushed itself to the forefront of her mind. "I've always wanted to live in a place like this," she said.

He paused half a step before continuing. "I guess that's a sign of your memory returning?"

"I guess. Trivial things seem to pop up when I'm not trying. Nothing helpful."

But it gave her hope that her memory would return on its own…eventually. She had to give her brain time to heal. Right now, she was more interested in learning about Jonah.

"Do you mind if I ask what was the unexpected news from your…ASAC, did you call him?"

"Yeah," Jonah confirmed. He heaved a sigh and slipped his hands into his front pockets. "I've been meaning to talk to you since you told Stella I'm an FBI agent."

Her eyes bulged. "Jonah, was I not supposed to say that?"

"Don't worry—you didn't know. It's not like we've had much time to discuss it."

"No wonder you didn't identify yourself as an agent to that park ranger or Sheriff Riley."

"It's complicated right now. Complicated and classified. I've been working undercover for a long time, earning trust and working my way to the top of a dangerous organization. Some things happened that could jeopardize the entire operation, so Chase, my ASAC, pulled me out and asked me to go off-grid."

"Sounds scary. Is that why you were at the cabin?"

"Yep." Jonah kicked a rock and sent it spinning. "I

inherited that old place a long time ago. Of course, I added a few special modifications along the way." He grinned at her.

"I think I would've started with indoor plumbing, but that's just me."

They both laughed. "Part of laying low means keeping my job and my face hidden for a while."

"The beard?"

He drew his hand over his whiskers. "Oh man, I can't wait to shave this thing off."

"I kinda like it."

His eyebrows shot up. "Really?"

"Well, now that you've, you know, showered and trimmed it close. It suits you." She smiled.

"Thank you. But listen, I really can't tell the entire town I'm FBI. Chase is briefing Sheriff Riley, but it's best to let everyone else assume I'm a local."

"Oh, but what about Stella?"

"I asked her to keep it to herself," he said. "Besides, she's letting two complete strangers stay in her home. Knowing I'm FBI is fair."

They followed the trail that wound around the edge of the lake. Belle eyed the patch of green algae on the surface of the water. A memory tried to surface, but it refused to form into something she could put into words. Was it connected to the lake where she was attacked? No, it wasn't the lake. It was the algae.

She had to refocus. Stop trying so hard to force the memories. Except, if she learned more about Jonah, maybe she could figure out why he seemed so familiar.

"You do remind me of someone, you know."

"Oh, yeah?"

"I can't figure it out. Something in your eyes. I think I know, then *poof*! It fades away."

He grinned. "Well, you remind me of someone too."

"Who?"

"My mom."

She barked a laugh. "Oh, perfect! Exactly what every girl wants to hear."

"No, I mean…" Jonah chuckled. "Your strength in dealing with everything. You've been through so much, and yet have a sense of humor about it. You're so strong."

"So, your mom is a strong woman?"

"Yes, she was. She raised me after my dad died. I don't know how she did it. She was the strongest person I've ever known." He glanced at her. "Until now."

Heat rushed to her cheeks, and she looked at her feet. "I don't know about your mom, but my strength comes from God."

Jonah sniffed.

She glanced at him. Now he was the one watching his feet move across the dirt path. Seemed like Jonah closed up each time she mentioned God. "What's with the grunt?"

"Let's just say, I'm glad God's on your side because He's sure never been on mine."

Before she could ask him to explain, Jonah caught her arm and stopped her from walking onto the road. Distracted by their conversation, she hadn't realized the trail ended. Maybe if they walked a while longer, Jonah would explain that comment about God not being on his side.

She nodded to the one lane bridge in the distance. "Think we can continue exploring?"

Jonah checked the road in both directions. "You sure you're up for it?"

No, she wasn't sure. If they continued walking, there was a good chance she'd pay for it later. But it was worth it to spend time getting to know the man who'd saved her life. "I think I can handle it."

"Okay, but remember, if we see other people I need to blend in," he said. "And tell me if you feel tired. We'll turn back."

They walked in silence until they reached the center of the bridge. Jonah paused and rested his elbows on the railing. Side by side, they took in the beauty of their surroundings. Towering fir trees lined the bank on both sides. Smooth wet rocks of all sizes forced the water to part into tiny rapids on their way downstream. Belle listened to the birds sing over the rippling water.

"I know I keep saying it," she sighed. "But I love it here. It's so peaceful."

"I might lose my man card for admitting this, but the views are breathtaking. There's something about the mountains I find restful. It's why I love my mountain refuge so far away from civilization. My own place of serenity when the job gets tough and I need to clear my head."

Belle cringed. "No hard feelings about your cabin?"

He draped an arm over her shoulder. "None at all."

"Even if it was a criminal who threw us together, I'm glad we met, Jonah."

He grinned. "I'm glad we met too, Belle."

The sound of an engine rumbled and they turned to see an old pickup rounding the bend in the road. The truck fishtailed coming out of the corner, but the driver regained control of his vehicle and kept coming fast.

Too fast.

Jonah tightened his arm around Belle's shoulder and pulled her close. They faced the speeding pickup truck. The driver must be a local who knew these roads all too well and didn't hesitate to exceed the speed limit. Unfortunately, he seemed oblivious to them. They were trapped on the narrow bridge with nowhere to go.

Jonah raised his arms over his head and waved. "Hey! Slow down, pal!"

The truck engine revved and he heard the distinct sound of the gears grinding into place. Instead of slowing, it picked up speed. Rocks clanged against the metal undercarriage. This guy was going to kill someone if he wasn't careful.

Jonah squinted but couldn't see a license plate on the front of the pickup. The sun glinted off the windshield and he could make out the outline of the driver with his fingers clutching the steering wheel, but a shadow obscured his face.

"He's not slowing, Jonah." Belle's voice quivered.

"I see that. We need to get off this bridge."

Jonah glanced over the railing. Water rushed over smooth gray boulders littering the stream. They could make the short drop, but not with those rocks. They'd break bones or shatter a skull on impact.

The truck barreled toward the bridge with no intention of stopping.

Jonah's blood ran cold. He grabbed Belle's shoulder and spun her around. "Run!"

They sprinted. Their feet pounded the wood slats, but his heart thudded faster than his feet could go. With his long legs, he could outrun Belle but no way he would leave her behind.

Twenty yards away and closing in. The end of the bridge still ten yards ahead of them. His brain attempted to calculate their chances. Not good.

"Faster," he breathed.

The truck growled and Jonah stole a glance over his shoulder. His toe caught the lip of a board and he tripped. Trying to keep his footing, he stumbled clumsily and lost his balance. His knee went down, driving into the solid plank. Pain flashed as his kneecap absorbed the impact.

Belle slowed.

"No! Keep going!"

He pushed to his feet and in a few strides, they were side by side again hurtling toward their only exit. The vehicle lurched forward with the roar of the engine on their heels. He had them cornered with no time for Jonah to go on the offense.

Jonah caught Belle's arm and she stabbed him with a panicked stare.

"Trust me," he said.

With his other arm, he scooped Belle up and carried her three long strides to the railing, ignoring the ache in his knee. The hood of the truck closed the remaining few yards.

Jonah jumped.

The narrow patch of grass alongside the bridge gave way to a steep drop. He crushed Belle to his chest. Covered her head with one hand to form a helmet of protection. Together, they skidded down the embankment with Jonah on his back holding Belle tightly. Rocks scraped his hamstring as he slid. His foot caught a jutting tree root, and they came to an abrupt halt at the edge of the water.

The high-pitched whine of brakes sent a chill down his spine. The driver stopped.

Jonah sat, holding Belle close to him. "We've got to keep moving. Can you stand?"

"Yeah, I think so," she panted.

He released Belle and she pulled herself into a crouch, holding a tree trunk for support. "Use the trees and rocks for cover but watch your step. Don't fall."

Belle nodded and pushed off the tree and into the next one. She ducked around it and glanced back at Jonah.

He motioned for her to keep moving and pulled his gun from the concealed holster. Through the foliage, he surveyed the truck. He could see the lower half, but no visual of the driver.

Engine idling, the truck rumbled at the end of the bridge. He had to get a look at this guy. Ignoring the soreness in his knee, Jonah picked his way over the muddy bank. Using the bridge as concealment, he hunched low and climbed toward the road.

Gravel flew in all directions as the driver stomped on the gas and the tires spun out. The truck did a dizzying one-eighty and fishtailed, the rear grinding against the metal railing. For a split second, sparks flew from the flank before the driver course-corrected and floored it. The truck's suspension bucked violently on the uneven wood deck as it sped away.

In a hushed voice, Jonah called to Belle, "Stay there. I think he left."

He pulled himself toward the road using the rocks and roots jutting from the ground, staying low. In the distance, Jonah heard the sound of a second vehicle. A quieter one. He ventured farther to the edge of the road and saw the sheriff's SUV approaching. Jonah glanced in the other direction, but the only sign of the pickup was a faint cloud of dust hovering over the road.

He scrambled to his feet and waved both arms over his head. "Hey! Sheriff Riley, right here!"

Red-and-blue emergency lights flashed on, and Jonah heaved a sigh. He turned, and after a moment of searching, located Belle. Only her fingertips and one eye visible at the tree where she hid.

"It's okay. The driver is gone, and the sheriff is here. Stay there and I'll help you up."

"No rush," she said, patting the trunk. "This tree and I are getting to know each other."

Jonah chuckled and shook his head. The woman made him laugh even when tensions were high. When his blood was prone to boil and he wanted to let off steam, somehow her humor cut the flame. He had to admit, he liked it.

Sheriff Riley slammed his door and jogged toward Jonah. "You guys all right? What happened?"

"A pickup tried to run us down. We jumped out of the way in time and rolled downhill." Jonah jerked his thumb over his shoulder. "I think you scared him off."

Riley looked past Jonah. "You okay, young lady?"

"Peachy," Belle said.

"Help her up here while I call my deputy. I was heading over to chat with you, so I'll drive you back to Stella's and you can give me your statement there."

Half an hour later, after Sheriff Riley photographed the tire tracks and sent his deputy to search for the truck, Jonah and Belle sat around Stella's dining room table with Riley. They drank iced tea from mason jars.

"I can't believe someone tried to run you over," Stella said. She applied antibiotic ointment and a clean bandage to Belle's stitches.

Jonah stared at the ice floating in his tea. Adopted. Why didn't his mom tell him? Did she think it would change his feelings for her? For his dad? Would it? He didn't even know.

"That was some quick thinking, jumping over the rail like that," Riley said.

Riley's statement drew Jonah back to the conversation. "Oh, yeah. It happened so fast—I didn't have time to draw my gun. Still can't believe I didn't get a look at the guy."

"This is all my fault," Belle said. "If I hadn't lost my stupid memory, I could tell you who is doing all this."

Jonah placed his hand over hers. "Don't blame yourself. This guy is unpredictable. He's reckless and he'll get caught."

"But no telling how much harm he'll do before that happens," Belle muttered.

Jonah saw a patrol vehicle similar to Sheriff Riley's pulling up the driveway.

"That's my deputy, Abe Lightfoot," Riley said. He stood and rapped his knuckles on the table. "I'll bring him in."

Through the window Jonah watched Deputy Lightfoot climb out of his vehicle and greet Riley with a chin lift. The deputy was shorter than Riley by several inches, but it was clear by his thick arms and broad chest the man worked out. His black hair was combed back and shone so much it appeared wet. How much hair product did it take to keep it in place? Deputy Lightfoot chatted with Riley for several minutes then they came inside.

Riley introduced the deputy and Jonah stood to shake his hand. "I'm Jonah Phillips and this is Belle."

"Nice to meet you both. Please call me Abe." His voice held a slight accent. "Sorry about your troubles. Things are usually much quieter around here."

Abe's dark eyes held Jonah's gaze for several seconds. Had Riley told him Jonah was an agent?

"Good to see you, Abe. Can I fix you some iced tea?" Stella asked.

"No, ma'am. I need to head back out. I wanted to inform these fine people that I've located the pickup. Looks like it was stolen from the Warwicks' ranch early this morning. We're processing it."

Riley shifted his weight. "At this point, we can't tell if

this is related to your attack, or just some bored kid out for a joy ride in his dad's truck."

Jonah scratched his beard. "I could be wrong, but I don't think a kid could pull that one-eighty."

"I'm with Jonah. I think it's the same guy and until my memory comes back, he's going to keep coming after me. Which means I'm putting everyone around me in danger," Belle said.

Stella put her arm around Belle's shoulder. "Oh, honey, don't you worry about that. There's more than enough security around here. We can protect you."

"Yeah, but who is going to protect *you*? I have to remember something about who I am. Something more than *I like coffee*, you know?"

Abe held up a finger. "Actually, ma'am. I've got an idea about that."

NINE

Belle stared at Deputy Abe Lightfoot, skeptical of any scheme he might offer to help her memory return. She was desperate to know her own identity, but so far, the best course of action seemed to be to wait. Let her brain heal and her memories pop up on their own. It seemed to be working, but it was taking too long.

Right now, her main concern was the attacker. What if he came for her at Stella's and set the house on fire while they slept? If Stella was hurt…well, Belle couldn't live with that.

She ran her finger over the water droplets sliding down the mason jar. "I'm not sure there's anything that can help at this point, Deputy."

Abe shifted. "Yes, ma'am. I empathize with your situation, but I wondered if you'd be willing to see a medical professional. Other than Dr. Park that is."

"I thought the landslide made that impossible," Jonah said.

"He means Dr. McGee," Riley said. "It slipped my mind because she…well, she doesn't come to town often."

"She's a bit of a hermit," Stella said. "Very nice woman, keeps to herself."

"And she's a doctor?" Belle asked.

"A psychiatrist. She only sees patients over the internet these days," Abe said. "I thought she might make an exception. If you're willing."

Belle looked at Jonah. "What do you think? Should I see a psychiatrist?"

Jonah blew out a breath. "Well, I can't see how it would hurt. What you really need is a hospital, but who knows? Maybe she can help?"

"Stella, what do you think?" Belle asked.

"I agree. It's worth a shot...*if* she will see you."

Belle caught the look Stella flashed to Sheriff Riley. What were they leaving out? Were Dr. McGee's methods questionable? No, these people had Belle's best interest in mind and wouldn't even suggest someone unless they trusted her.

"Okay then." Belle exhaled. "I'll try almost anything at this point."

"I'll give her a call and see if she is willing," Riley said. "You get some rest while we keep working this case. I'll be in touch."

"Thank you both," Belle said, nodding to Riley and Abe. "Rest sounds great. I think I'll head upstairs for a nap if you don't mind."

Stella rose from the table with Belle. "We don't mind at all, sweetheart. Can I get you anything? How's your pain?"

"I'm a little sore, but nothing a rest can't help." She gave Stella a hug.

Jonah walked her upstairs and leaned against the doorjamb, arms folded. "We're going to catch this guy, Belle. It's only a matter of time."

"I know." She flopped on the bed and offered Jonah a flat smile. "If I could remember—"

"Rest," he interrupted. "It will help."

"I think I need to hibernate at this point."

He grinned. "Sleep as long as your body will let you. Don't worry about us. We'll be here when you wake."

Belle watched Jonah leave, as he closed the door all but an inch behind him. Knowing he was near helped her relax. His quick thinking had prevented the truck from running them over. He was strong and smart, and he would continue to keep her safe.

She reached for the Bible and read until she drifted off.

Nightmares of running through the forest disrupted her sleep. The attacker on her heels with arms outstretched. Every step weighted and holding her back. She couldn't get her feet to move fast enough. Her lungs burned and refused to provide enough oxygen. The man stepped into her path, and she screamed. Blurry features came into focus and revealed a face.

The face of Jonah.

A strong hand grasped her shoulder and gave her a gentle shake. A familiar voice urging her to wake up. The hand on her shoulder wasn't part of the dream. Someone was in the room with her. Sleep tried to pull her back under, but she fought against it and forced her eyes open.

Jonah.

"You're okay," he whispered.

Belle tried to orient herself. "What…where am I?"

"Don't worry. You're safe. We're at Stella's house. I heard you cry out and came to check on you."

"Were you having a bad dream?" Stella asked from the doorway.

Belle sat up and rubbed her eyes. "A nightmare." She threw the covers back and climbed out of bed.

"Here, I brought you some hot tea." Stella placed a small tray on the nightstand and sat on the edge of the bed. "Do you want to talk about it?"

She drew in a breath. "In my dream, the attacker caught

me. It was all blurry, but when I screamed, he came into focus, and I saw him. I saw his face." Belle paused and met Jonah's gaze.

"Did you recognize him?" he asked.

"Yeah." She hesitated. Her mouth went dry, and she swallowed.

Jonah and Stella exchanged a curious look.

"What did you see," Jonah asked.

"I saw… I saw…*you*."

"Belle…I…I…never—"

"I know, I know." Belle took Jonah's hand. "It was a dream. My head is all jumbled and I'm mixing events. I know that."

A chime rang out and Stella rose. "That's my patient. Belle, are you sure you're okay?"

"Yes, thank you for the tea."

"My pleasure. I'll be in the barn if you need me. Shouldn't be long."

When Stella left, Jonah took Belle's other hand. "You know I would never hurt you like that, right?"

"Yes, I know." She groaned. "This whole thing is a mess. I don't understand how I got to this point. A man trying to kill me? And for what? I can't even remember my own name, or where I live!"

She looked at Jonah. "Because of me, you lost your home and you're forced to stay here with strangers."

Tears slid from the corners of her eyes and Jonah used his thumb to catch them.

"You didn't cause this, Belle. I'm not *forced* to stay here. I'm choosing to stay." He stroked her hair away from her face. Their eyes locked. "I'll do everything I can to protect you. I'm not leaving until you're no longer in danger."

Belle's pulse quickened at his touch and the way his

voice fell to a husky whisper. She bit her lower lip and watched his pupils dilate. Her hand moved to his chest before she could stop it. Not to push him away. To feel his warmth.

His heart thundered beneath her palm and her own pulse raced at the sensation. What would it be like to kiss him right here, right now?

Jonah dropped his eyes to her mouth and leaned into her hand, closing the distance between them. Her heart rate kicked up another notch as Jonah cupped her jaw.

The sound of the door chime sliced through the moment and Jonah pulled away so fast her hand fell from his chest. He blinked, and for a moment she thought he might kiss her anyway.

"I'm so sorry," he said, stepping back.

"Jonah, wait—"

Before she could finish, he was out the door.

Belle collapsed onto the bed and blew out a breath. In the moment, she'd wanted nothing more than to have his strong arms wrapped around her. And if he'd kissed her, she wouldn't have pushed him away. But deep down, she knew it wasn't right. Not here. Not yet.

Still, her stomach fluttered at the thought of kissing Jonah.

Jonah stopped halfway down the stairs and pressed his back against the wall. What was he thinking? He almost kissed Belle. If the door hadn't chimed, would he have?

What he'd done was wrong on so many levels. Belle needed his protection, not his advances. With her amnesia preventing her from remembering who she was, he could be putting her in an awful situation. She could have a boyfriend. Or worse, she could be married. If he'd kissed her, well, how could she explain the betrayal to her husband? He didn't want to think about how awful it would be. He didn't think she was in a relationship, but then how would he know? Either way, he didn't want to put her in that situation.

He couldn't deny his feelings for the woman. She was a firecracker for sure. From her wild red hair to her spunky personality, she was everything he'd never known he wanted. But getting close to her was playing with fire. One more reason to keep his heart in check.

"Knock, knock." The voice of Sheriff Riley floated upstairs.

"Coming," Jonah said.

He jogged the remaining few steps and rounded the corner to see Riley waiting in the kitchen.

"How's Belle doing?" Riley asked.

"She had a nightmare, so I was just checking on her. Other than that, she's doing great—I guess." Jonah crossed his arms "What about you? Any news?"

"Good news and bad news. Good news is, I was able to reach Dr. McGee and she will see Belle tomorrow morning. That is, if you think Belle wants to go."

"I'll double-check. It's really her only option unless the road is passable?"

Riley grimaced. "Not yet. They've cleared several other roads, the higher-trafficked ones, but they won't make it up to us until tomorrow at the earliest. Probably take them most of the day to get it back to a place where we can safely drive."

Jonah knew how long clearing and rebuilding the smaller dirt roads could take. The narrowness made it difficult if not impossible to get heavy-duty equipment up the mountain. They'd need to use manual labor to clear the landslide debris, then verify the stability of the road before allowing people to travel.

"So, that's the bad news?" Jonah asked.

"It wasn't the bad news I was talking about, but yeah."

"No prints on the truck?"

Riley shook his head. "Wiped clean."

"Figures." Jonah shook his head.

If the attacker knew they'd be on the road, then somewhere out there, the evil man waited. Watched. Heat flushed Jonah's neck. Time to be proactive. Set a trap. Catch him before he attacked again.

"Now what do we do?" Belle asked.

Jonah glanced over to see her strolling barefoot into the kitchen. Lost in thought, he hadn't heard her come down the stairs. No good. He'd have to be more alert.

"We'll keep investigating," Riley said. "Question the locals and find a witness if we can. In this town, few things go unnoticed. I informed Jonah about Dr. McGee. You're all set to see her tomorrow morning, first thing if you still want."

"Thank you, Sheriff," Belle said. "I do, but how will we get there? We don't have a car."

"I spoke with Stella while you were asleep," Jonah said. "She offered to let us take her old work truck and gave me directions."

Belle's eyes drifted past Jonah into a blank stare. Was she worried about being alone with Jonah after he'd nearly kissed her? No, he was being silly. The disappointment in her eyes when he pulled away said she sensed the chemistry between them too. She worried about driving to Dr. McGee's house with an assailant stalking her.

Jonah crossed to Belle and touched her elbow. "You okay?"

She startled. "What? Oh, yeah, I'm good. I was thinking about the dream."

"Did you remember something else?" Jonah asked.

"No. Well, maybe." She absently ran a finger under the stitches on her forehead, the bandage no longer covering the wound. "I don't know if it's a memory or a dream, but I remember something... Something about algae."

Jonah exchanged a look with Riley. "Algae? You mean the mold that grows on water?"

"It's not mold—it's a plant." Belle's eyes widened at her own words, then she furrowed her brow. "Does that mean anything? Isn't it common knowledge?"

"Not to me," Riley said.

"Me, either." Jonah pulled on his beard. "It could be related to your job. Are you a teacher? Maybe you teach biology?"

"Earlier, a laboratory flashed to mind, so maybe." She furrowed her brow. "I really can't remember. For all I know, I'm an algae farmer."

"I've met people with worse jobs," Riley said.

"You know what? I'll save all the speculating for tomorrow with Dr. McGee. Anyone need a glass of tea?"

"That'd be great," Jonah said.

Riley's police duty belt creaked as he leaned half on, half off the counter stool. "I can't stay long, but I'll take one if you're making."

Jonah watched Belle move in the kitchen, her motions lithe and unhitched. After all the physical trauma she'd endured, she didn't appear to be in pain. His own muscles were stiff and sore, especially when he tried to stand up after sitting. The bruise on his knee wasn't too bad, but the bullet graze on his side burned if he twisted or moved wrong. A nagging reminder of the very real danger they were in until they uncovered the man stalking Belle. But Belle's emotional state was his biggest concern, one he hoped Dr. McGee would help with tomorrow.

"So, Sheriff Riley," Belle said, dropping ice cubes into mason jars. "How long have you known Stella?"

Jonah was glad Belle asked the question, because he wondered about their relationship too. They seemed close, and the way Riley looked at Stella said they had history.

"A while," he said.

"Really? Did you both grow up around here?" Belle asked.

Riley shifted. "Not really."

Jonah raised his eyebrows. Belle shrugged and delivered their tea. They each took a sip to fill the awkward silence.

The door chimed and Jonah turned to see Stella coming through the back entrance.

She stopped to kick off her boots and smiled when she saw them. "Hey, good to see you're out of bed, Belle. Glad to see you too, Linc."

She moved to the sink and turned the tap on to wash her hands. "So, what're we talking about?"

"Belle was just asking the sheriff about how you guys know each other," Jonah said.

Stella cut the water and put all her focus into drying her hands. "Oh, and what did he say?"

Riley drummed the counter and stood. "Actually, I was about to head out. Let's save that story for another day."

"Good idea," Stella said.

"I need to get back to the investigation, so I'll catch up with you guys later."

With that, Riley left.

Jonah flicked a gaze at Stella.

Stella sighed and refolded the hand towel. "He's a busy man, that sheriff." Stella clapped her hands and pasted on a smile. "You two go wash up and I'll start dinner."

TEN

Belle bounced on the bench seat next to Jonah as he drove the switchbacks in a steady climb up the mountain to Dr. McGee's. The old farm truck Stella loaned them squeaked and groaned over every bump. Was the road made of dirt-covered boulders? No wonder Dr. McGee rarely drove to Piney Village. Belle couldn't imagine a vehicle's suspension surviving this drive more than a few times before key parts began to fall off.

At least Belle was short. Poor Jonah's head banged into the roof of the pickup each time it bounced over a rock. Thankful for the seat belt holding her down, she used both hands to brace herself on the dash and craned her neck to see if anyone followed them. So far, the road was deserted. They hadn't passed another vehicle during the drive.

"How much farther?" Her words vibrated on the way out.

"Almost there." Jonah glanced at her and grinned. "It's a little rough, huh?"

"I'd answer that question, but I'm afraid we'll hit a rock and I'll bite my tongue off."

Jonah barked a laugh, and she noted the soft smile lines in the corners of his eyes. She liked them. She liked *him*. But the attraction was more than physical. Circumstances had thrown them together, and despite her initial fear of him, she'd come to see him as the honorable man he really was.

"Boy that was weird with Riley and Stella last night, wasn't it?" he said.

"Yeah, evasive much?"

He chuckled. "That's what I thought. I could learn a thing or two from him about dodging the simplest questions."

"I don't think you'd want to mimic that act. Anyone could see right through him. There's definitely something going on there."

"Maybe he's undercover?" Jonah shot her a glance.

"It's more common than you'd think," she teased.

Jonah braked and pointed. "Look, I think that's the place."

A barbwire fence ran the length of a meadow with a narrow break wide enough to allow a vehicle through. The native grass grew high and almost obscured the beaten-down tire tracks. If Jonah hadn't pointed it out, she would've missed it.

He eased the truck through the opening in the fence and followed the rutted driveway to a log cabin with a wraparound porch. A woman in a sun hat worked in a garden of raised beds near the home. When she saw them, she rose and dusted the dirt off her knees. She pulled her gloves off and used them to direct Jonah to park alongside the house.

Belle climbed out of the truck and braced herself against the door. Solid ground. It took a second for her brain to register the steady surface, and for a moment she swayed.

Dr. McGee strode toward them, removing her hat to reveal silky black hair shimmering in the morning sunlight. Her crystal-blue eyes and pale skin didn't fit her long dark hair, but Belle found the contrast lovely.

"You must be Jonah and Belle. Glad you found the place," she said. "I was afraid you'd get lost and wander around the mountain until you ran out of gas."

"It's a pleasure to meet you, Dr. McGee," Belle said.

"Oh, call me Rebecca, please. We're all friends here. Come on inside so we can get started."

"If you'll excuse me, I'm going to stay on the porch and make a few calls while I have coverage." Jonah waved his satellite phone.

Belle nodded and gave him a thin smile before following Rebecca inside. The house was minimally furnished. It was clean and neat with few personal items visible anywhere. She looked for family photographs but didn't notice any.

Rebecca led Belle into a room that appeared to be a formal dining room turned into a comfortable office. A hand-carved wooden desk with a wide computer monitor as the centerpiece faced the window. Overstuffed bookshelves lined the opposite wall. No photos in this room, either.

Rebecca closed the French doors and gestured to an oversize leather chair. "You can sit here."

Belle took the offered seat and glanced out the window beside the chair. A thick forest stretched behind the house. "This is cozy."

Rebecca pulled her office chair closer and sat. "I apologize for the informality. I don't see patients in person. It's all done online these days."

"It must get lonely," Belle said.

Rebecca considered her. "I imagine you know something about that yourself."

"What do you mean?"

"Isn't it rather lonely not knowing who you are or where you're from?"

Okay. Dr. McGee was good. She'd flipped the conversation and zeroed in on Belle's issues like a master.

Belle nodded. "It is. Except I have Jonah. Sort of."

"Sheriff Riley explained your situation to me, but I'd like to hear it from you if you don't mind."

"Okay, but it might take a while."

Rebecca loosely gestured to the room around them. "I've got nowhere else to be, so please take all the time you need."

Belle spent the next several minutes recounting everything she could remember, pausing only to answer Rebecca's clarifying questions. When she finished, Rebecca stood and walked to the window. She clasped her hands behind her back and stared at the trees in silence.

Belle waited.

A few moments passed and Rebecca returned to her seat. "It sounds to me like you have retrograde amnesia. This could be brought on by your head injury, or the traumatic incidents you suffered. Or it could be caused by both. You certainly need to see a physician, but I believe we need to retrieve a single foundational memory in order to trigger more. It could take months of therapy. Or if you'll agree, we can try something called eye movement desensitization and reprocessing, or EMDR therapy as it's more commonly referred to."

"EMDR? What's that?"

"With EMDR, I can attempt to help you connect to a repressed memory. You'll be aware and actively participating, so we can stop at any time. It may not work, but I'd like to try it if you're willing."

Belle studied the doctor's features. Her kind eyes told Belle she could trust the woman. Besides, it would be so nice to learn who she was. Even something as small as her real name would be worth it.

Her sigh was deep. "Okay, Doctor, what do we do?"

Rebecca explained the EMDR therapy technique and what to expect. It sounded a little farfetched, but Belle was desperate. After an hour of following a moving light for a while, then pausing to talk, Belle could visualize the attack in the woods with more clarity.

"I had a backpack."

"Good, Belle. Now tell me why you were going to the lake."

"Algae," she breathed. An image of the lake materialized. "For research. I...I had a research project."

"That's good, Belle."

They continued, but no matter how hard she tried, Belle couldn't remember her name or where she worked. It was infuriating.

Rebecca clicked off the penlight. "That's enough for now."

She followed along with the breathing exercise Rebecca used to end the session. Belle's muscles relaxed and her spotty vision returned to normal.

Standing, Belle then moved to the window and stretched her stiff muscles. "Algae, hmm. That explains my fascination with the algae I saw on Piney Lake."

"Well, there can't be too many algae scientists around here. I have an idea." Rebecca spun her chair around to face the computer. She wiggled her mouse, and the screen came to life. "Your attack happened near Eagle Lake, not Piney Lake, right?"

"Yeah, that's right."

Rebecca typed *algae research Eagle Lake* into a search engine and watched the results pop up.

Belle leaned over Rebecca's shoulder and read as she

scrolled through the first page of the results. "Anything stand out to you?"

"Nope, not a thing."

Rebecca tilted her head to peer around her monitor. "Is that Jonah way over there?"

Belle glanced out the window to see the silhouette of a man standing among the trees, feet planted shoulder-width apart. She waved, but he disappeared behind the house.

"We've been in here for a while, so he must've decided to explore."

"We won't be much longer. I want to try something else," Rebecca said.

Belle returned her attention to the computer.

Rebecca clicked on the image search, and the screen filled with photos. "Let's look at these. We may find a photo you recognize."

"Or a photo of *me*!" Belle pointed.

In the photo, Belle stood with four men, surrounded by lab equipment. Her heart nearly exploded at the sight of herself in safety goggles and a white lab coat.

"There! Look! My name is embroidered on my lab coat. I can't read it. What does it say?"

"Let me enlarge the image."

Even with the photo enlarged, Belle couldn't read the writing. "Click the link to the article. My name *has* to be there."

"It says here, 'a research grant was awarded to Dr. Robert Winn for his award-winning research on cyanobacteria,'" Rebecca read.

Belle barely registered Rebecca's words. Her eyes zeroed in on the caption beneath the group photo naming each scientist. The third name lined up with her position in the photograph. It was the only female name in the caption.

Dr. Belinda Lewis.

* * *

Belinda Lewis.

Jonah turned the name over and over in his mind on the drive back to Stella's house. He drove slower this time. Easing them over the mountainous terrain to avoid the jostling they endured on the way up. His bones still rattled from the trip earlier. Besides, driving down a mountain with switchback turns was always dangerous. Even more so on a gravel road.

Belinda. The name didn't fit after calling her Belle for so long. Could he still use the nickname? Maybe she'd want to go by Belinda to reaffirm her identity? He stole a glance across the pickup at the courageous woman who seemed to take his breath away every time he looked at her. Belle gazed out the window, chin resting on her fist.

Questions popped off in his mind like firecrackers. He wanted a debrief of the entire session but after they left Dr. McGee, Belle seemed pensive, and he didn't want to intrude on her privacy. They'd filled him in on the basics of how they discovered her true name, but not much else.

"You can call me Belle, you know." The comment seemed to be plucked right from his thoughts. Belle adjusted her seat belt and angled her body to face him.

He couldn't stop the grin. "Good, I like calling you Belle."

Her cheeks flushed red, and she dipped her head. "That moment when I saw my name, well, it didn't trigger a flood of memories like I imagined it would. Rebecca says with rest and time, my memories may return on their own, but some might be gone forever."

Gone forever? The idea made his stomach lurch. To forget your past life and never know what events sculpted and shaped your identity? It seemed parts of his life were missing too.

While Belle was with Rebecca, Jonah called Chase and confirmed his parents never told him he was adopted. Chase apologized for dropping the news in his lap that way, but Jonah didn't mind. No matter how painful, he'd rather have facts immediately.

Chase said he was tracking down Jonah's birth records. Until then, Jonah didn't want to focus on his past. He'd rather help Belle with hers.

"So, this *Belinda*... What do you remember about *her*?"

Belle hitched a shoulder. "Betrayal."

He flicked his eyes to hers, then back to the road. Did she mean him? There were things he had to keep hidden, things he simply couldn't tell her. Not until his name was cleared. But he would never intentionally hurt her. "Who betrayed you?"

"My colleague, Dr. Robert Winn. He pretended to be interested in me romantically, only to get close to me and steal my research."

"Ah." The tension in his shoulders eased. "I guess that means you're not married or in a relationship."

Belle laughed softly. "No, I'm not."

The confident reply pleased him. "What research did this Winn guy steal?"

"My memory is hazy about the science behind the project, but the day we posed for that photograph, I remember fuming the whole time because he claimed my years of research as his own."

"Did you confront him about it?"

"I must have, but I don't recall." She chewed her lower lip, a habit of concentration he found adorable.

"And it was your research that put you on the hiking trail the day we met." He grimaced. "You know what I mean."

"I think I was testing algae on the lake. Again, it's all fuzzy."

"Well, Riley can check it out. He'll find your car and should be able to track your movements. Find the area where you were first attacked and uncover a clue."

"I remembered I had a backpack. It's still out there unless the attacker took it." She pinched the bridge of her nose. "Can we talk about you for a while? Do you mind?"

"Me?" he laughed. "What's there to know about me?"

"Before that guy tried to run us down. You were going to tell me about your mom."

"Ahhh, yes."

Should he tell Belle about the bombshell Chase dropped yesterday? Really, he was still trying to process it himself. Adopted? It must be a mistake. No, he wouldn't tell Belle until he had proof.

Jonah slowed the truck and concentrated on navigating a hairpin curve. "Mom was a trauma nurse in the emergency room. She quit after I was born and never went back to work. I barely remember my dad. He was a detective. Undercover. Always working.

"When I was nine, she got really sick. Breast cancer. In the midst of her battle, my dad was shot and killed."

"Oh, Jonah. That's horrible." She gave his bicep a reassuring squeeze. "Can I ask what happened?"

He stole a glance at Belle. She'd shifted and angled her hips to him. Everything about this woman enraptured him. Smart, caring and with the uncanny ability to make him laugh, she took all the pressure off. He could be himself around her. But that was a problem.

A problem that could get him killed.

"The wiretaps revealed that during an undercover operation my dad slipped. Distracted by his personal problems, he broke undercover character. Mentioned his wife had breast cancer to the wrong guy. The mistake cost him his life."

He worked his jaw muscles and steered around another sharp corner. Jonah struggled with this part of the job too. Every time he walked into a room as an undercover agent, he put lives on the line. Not just his, but his team and anyone close to him. The risk of slipping out of his undercover persona or saying the wrong thing weighed heavy on his shoulders and took a toll mentally and physically. He couldn't let his personal life become a distraction. Not ever again.

"They shot him in the stomach and left him to die in the desert. I was just a kid, but I sat in the hospital waiting room and prayed with Mom. The look on the surgeon's face told me God hadn't heard our prayers."

"God heard your prayers, Jonah."

"I know," he interrupted. No platitudes or discussion about *God's plan*. He'd heard it enough times during his childhood to last a lifetime. "So, yeah…Mom fought the cancer for years, but it continued to spread. She died while I was at Quantico for new agent training."

A lump formed in his throat, and he choked it down. After all this time, the grief of losing his mother still left an ache in his chest. He would always regret not being there when it really counted for her and for—

A car coming up behind the truck caught Jonah's attention. The hair on the back of his neck prickled. They hadn't seen a car all day and now a white sedan appeared out of nowhere. After the encounter on the bridge, he was on high alert.

Belle reached over and placed her hand on his shoulder. The touch of her delicate fingers caressing his neck helped his muscles relax. "I'm really sorry about your

Enjoying Your Book?

Start saving on new books like the one you're reading with the *Harlequin Reader Service!*

Your first books are 100% Free!

See inside for more details

Get Free Books In Just 3 Easy Steps

Are you an avid reader searching for more books?
The **Harlequin Reader Service** might be for you! We'd love to send you up to **4 free books** just for trying it out. Just write **"YES"** on the **Free Books Voucher Card** and we'll send your free books and a gift, altogether worth over $20.

Step 1: Choose your Books

Try *Love Inspired® Romance Larger-Print* and get 2 books and fall in love with inspirational romances that take you on an uplifting journey of faith, forgiveness and hope.

Try *Love Inspired® Suspense Larger-Print* and get 2 books where courage and optimism unite in stories of faith and love in the face of danger.

Or *TRY BOTH*!

Step 2: Return your completed Free Books Voucher Card

Step 3: Receive your books and continue reading!

Your free books are **completely free**, even the shipping! If you continue with your subscription, you can look forward to curated monthly shipments of brand-new books from your selected series, always at a discount off the cover price! Plus you can cancel any time.

Don't miss out, reply today! Over $20 FREE value.

Free Books Voucher Card

▼ DETACH AND MAIL CARD TODAY! ▼

YES! I love reading, please send me more books from the series I'd like to explore and a free gift from each series I select.

More books are just 3 steps away!

Just write in "**YES**" on the dotted line below then select your series and return this Books Voucher today and we'll send your free books & a gift asap!

Choose your books:

- [ ] **Love Inspired® Romance Larger-Print** 122/322 CTI G29D
- [ ] **Love Inspired® Suspense Larger-Print** 107/307 CTI G29D
- [ ] **BOTH** 122/322 & 107/307 CTI G29F

FIRST NAME

LAST NAME

ADDRESS

APT.#

CITY

STATE/PROV.

ZIP/POSTAL CODE

EMAIL ❑ Please check this box if you would like to receive newsletters and promotional emails from Harlequin Enterprises ULC and its affiliates. You can unsubscribe anytime.

Your Privacy – Your information is being collected by Harlequin Enterprises ULC, operating as Harlequin Reader Service. For a complete summary of the information we collect, how we use this information and to whom it is disclosed, please visit our privacy notice located at https://corporate.harlequin.com/privacy-notice. From time to time we may also exchange your personal information with reputable third parties. If you wish to opt out of this sharing of your personal information, please visit www.readerservice.com/consumerschoice or call 1-800-873-8635. **Notice to California Residents** – Under California law, you have specific rights to control and access your data. For more information on these rights and how to exercise them, visit https://corporate.harlequin.com/california-privacy.

LI/LIS-1123-OM_123ST

© 2023 HARLEQUIN ENTERPRISES ULC
™ and ® are trademarks owned by Harlequin Enterprises ULC. Printed in the U.S.A.

HARLEQUIN Reader Service —**Here's how it works:**

Accepting your 2 free books and free gift (gift valued at approximately $10.00 retail) places you under no obligation to buy anything. You may keep the books and gift and return the shipping statement marked "cancel." If you do not cancel, approximately one month later we'll send you 6 more books from each series you have chosen, and bill you at our low, subscribers-only discount price. Love Inspired® Romance Larger-Print books and Love Inspired® Suspense Larger-Print books consist of 6 books each month and cost just $6.49 each in the U.S. or $6.74 each in Canada. That is a savings of at least 13% off the cover price. It's quite a bargain! Shipping and handling is just 50¢ per book in the U.S. and $1.25 per book in Canada*. You may return any shipment at our expense and cancel at any time by contacting customer service — or you may continue to receive monthly shipments at our low, subscribers-only discount price plus shipping and handling.

▲ If offer card is missing write to: Harlequin Reader Service, P.O. Box 1341, Buffalo, NY 14240-8531 or visit www.ReaderService.com ▲

BUSINESS REPLY MAIL
FIRST-CLASS MAIL   PERMIT NO. 717   BUFFALO, NY

POSTAGE WILL BE PAID BY ADDRESSEE

HARLEQUIN READER SERVICE
PO BOX 1341
BUFFALO NY 14240-8571

NO POSTAGE
NECESSARY
IF MAILED
IN THE
UNITED STATES

parents." Compassion and empathy filled her voice. "Is this why you don't think God is on your side?"

He darted his eyes from the rearview mirror to Belle before returning his gaze to the road. The car hung back.

"I guess I don't see the point of praying if it doesn't change things." The memory of Amy surged forward in his mind and with it a deep pang in his stomach. He didn't want to think about his college girlfriend, especially not now. How could he tell Belle about losing the woman he loved? And all because he wasn't there.

A brain-jarring impact from behind thrust Jonah against the steering wheel. The seat belt caught and clotheslined him. In the mirror, he saw the white car on their bumper. For a split second he thought it was accidental. The other driver inched closer. Jonah hit the gas, but the car closed the distance. In a crunch of plastic and metal, the car plowed into the tailgate again. The collision jarred Jonah and he realized the driver planned to run them off the road.

Nerves blazing with adrenaline, Jonah yelled, "Get down!"

"Jonah, what's happening?" Belle shouted.

He pushed the gas harder and swerved to the left lane, hugging the mountain to avoid the steep drop on their right.

"He's right behind us. Coming up on my side," Belle said. "I can't see his face! He's wearing a mask!"

"Belle, get down. He could have a gun!"

Instead of ducking below the dash, Belle laid across the seat and pressed her head against his thigh.

"Loop your arm through your seat belt," he shouted.

The smaller car gained speed and pulled along the passenger side. It crashed into the truck, pinning them against the mountain. A gritty grinding screech came from Jonah's door as it scraped along jutting rocks. He forced the accelerator to the floor. Pulled ahead and swerved into the right lane again. The mirror on Belle's door clipped the yellow road sign warning of a sharp corner. A hairpin turn in the road leading downhill to the next switchback.

They'd never make the turn at this speed.

He downshifted and relaxed the accelerator. Watched the mirror for a glimpse of the driver. It never came. The masked driver kept pace in Jonah's blind spot on the left. The driver knew Jonah had to enter the turn from the outside lane and he tried to block him.

No way, buddy. Not happening.

Jonah yanked the steering wheel. Crossed into the left lane and smashed into the smaller vehicle. The driver swerved right aiming to hit the truck again. It missed and veered off the road. The tires hit the narrow shoulder and skidded to a stop on loose gravel.

The distance allowed Jonah to slow before taking the hard right curve in the outside lane. The mountain dropped away, replaced by a guardrail that hugged the left side of the road. Coming into the turn, Jonah hit the brakes at the exact moment the front tire hit a rock in the road and exploded with a bang. A grunt escaped from Belle.

The steering wheel didn't respond. The truck plowed into the railing. Jonah regained control but it was too late. The guardrail gave way in a violent screech of tearing metal.

In a heart-fluttering moment he knew. It was out of his hands. He couldn't stop them from going over.

"Hold on, Bel—"

ELEVEN

A gritty metallic sound sliced through Jonah's words and pierced Belle's ears. The truck's left quarter panel shrieked against the guardrail twisting the thin barrier. The safety rail snapped, tearing away from the mountain.

She remembered she used to imagine this scenario while driving. A nagging *what-if* in the back of her mind while navigating these treacherous roads. Only a thin metal barrier separated vehicles from dropping off the mountain and she always knew it could happen. In fact, it was happening right now. The truck tipped and ice shot through her veins.

They were going over.

Jonah flung himself over her, arms raised to form a protective cocoon around her body. With her head covered, she couldn't see but she could hear. Tree limbs scratched and clawed at the pickup in an intense shriek. Branches cracked and snapped under the force of their truck plunging down the mountain. Her every sense heightened but everything happened too fast for her brain to fully process.

Gravity took control and yanked Jonah and Belle toward the driver's door. Her hips burned against the seat belt and her body slipped from the webbing a fraction, but it held. Jonah's head smacked against the window.

The truck tipped at a forty-five degree angle. Then time sped up and she caught glimpses of her world as she spiraled upside down.

She gasped as the vehicle twisted and rolled. Crashing through saplings and brush with rage. The truck collided with something hard and unmovable bringing them to an abrupt stop. The force flung Belle sideways, and a cold, solid surface grazed her forearm. The cut stung but she barely registered the pain. Only the deafening silence punctuated by a powerful hiss.

Belle sagged, held by the restraint locked against her lap. Despite it being early afternoon, the cab appeared dark. She strained to reach the buckle release but from her odd angle it was challenging. When her fingers found the button, she fumbled then pressed. The latch released and she dropped shoulder first to the roof of the truck.

"Jonah." She shook his shoulder. "Jonah, we have to get out of here."

He didn't respond. His limp body slumped against his restraint. Arms hanging over his head.

"No, no, no! Jonah!" She felt his neck for a pulse. A steady beat threaded against her fingers. "Thank You, God," she whispered.

If they stayed here much longer, the attacker would find them. With shaking hands, she managed to release Jonah's seat belt. His body dropped but he didn't wake. Belle patted his cheeks.

"Wake up, Jonah. C'mon! Wake up."

No response.

She took a moment to check their surroundings. Jonah's side of the truck hit the ground when they rolled. The vehicle rotated onto the roof and crashed into a rounded mass of rock on the passenger side. No way she could exit from her window. Besides the boulder blocking it, the entire door and a corner of the roof was crushed inward. The protective film on the windshield did its job and held the shattered glass together. A fallen tree covered the hood. At least the old truck didn't have airbags to struggle with.

Belle heard a noise and her breath caught. She stilled and listened.

Footsteps sliding on gravel.

"Jonah, he's coming! Wake up! You have to move!"

He groaned and his head lolled.

Fine. He'd saved her, and now it was her turn to save him. Bracing herself against the dash, she turned and kicked the back window. After three hard kicks she realized it was taking too long. She could crawl through the tiny sliding window but no way Jonah could fit. A quick survey of the truck didn't turn up anything she could use to smash the glass. Jonah's shirt rode up and his gun peeked out of his holster. Should she shoot the window? Smash it with the butt of his gun? No, too dangerous.

An idea sparked and she quickly removed the headrest. Instead of swinging it at the window, she pressed the metal rods into the corner of the rear windshield. She closed her eyes and leaned all her weight into it. The glass shattered. She turned the headrest around and used the soft end to clear away the broken shards.

"What happ—"

"Jonah!" She dropped the headrest and flung her arms around him. Without thinking, she pressed her lips to his as if it was the most natural thing in the world. His hand touched her waist, and she drew back. "Let's go. He's coming."

Jonah's glassy eyes tried to focus. He leaned forward with a soft groan. She studied him but he waved her away. "I'm fine. Groggy, but fine."

Belle crawled through the broken rear window then turned and helped Jonah drag himself out. He fell onto his back, hands on his chest. With the vehicle upside down, the bed of the truck offered some protection. She gave Jonah a once-over, but only saw minor cuts and scrapes.

He tried to move and winced. "Is this…is this how you felt?"

"If you're hurting now, wait until Stella sees her truck," she teased.

Jonah attempted a laugh, but it turned into a cough. He wiped his mouth with the back of his hand and pulled his phone from his pocket. "Here, call the sheriff. It's the last number I dialed."

"Okay, then we move." Belle found Riley's number and listened for him to answer. Sirens wailed in the distance. Was help already on the way?

"Jonah, you guys okay? I got a call about a truck going over the guardrail." Riley spoke over the sirens in the background.

"Sheriff, it's Belle," she interrupted. "A man in a white sedan rammed into us and sent us over. The truck flipped, but we're fine. We're hiding underneath the wreckage, but he's still out there."

A gunshot popped. The metallic clang sounded near the cab of the truck and echoed. Belle flinched and before she could think, Jonah threw himself over her. She wrapped her arms around his back and clung to his shirt. He slipped his gun from his holster and held it over her head.

They froze. Waiting. Listening. The rise and fall of Jonah's chest matched her own rapid breaths. Faint words echoed from the phone somewhere on the ground. Her shaky fingers groped until she found it and put it to her ear.

"Belle! Jonah! What's happening?" Riley yelled. "I heard gunshots."

"He's shooting the truck and we're trapped," she whispered. "Hurry!"

"Five minutes."

Gunfire blasted as the assailant raked the truck with bullets with the unmistakable staccato rhythm of a gunman draining his magazine.

Deafening blasts of gunfire inside the metal truck burned Jonah's eardrums. He tensed, tightening his muscles in anticipation of bullets tearing his flesh. Instead, the rounds punched through the steel truck bed. Each slug whizzed over their heads and lodged itself into the opposite side of their metal hiding place.

Jonah didn't dare move. They'd narrowly escaped the bullets zipping over them by mere inches. He needed to hold on a bit longer. Keep Belle safe until the sheriff arrived. Or, at the very least, until the attacker ran out of ammo. What he really wanted to do was crawl out and sight his own gun at the criminal and put this to an end. Right here, right now. Could he?

He flicked his gaze to the narrow gap between the ground and the upside-down vehicle. No way he could squeeze under there. Even Belle couldn't twist or contort her small frame through. The only option was to crawl through the broken back glass again and that would make him a sitting duck.

No, a fish. Fish in a barrel. The idiom struck Jonah and his chest heaved with a contained laugh.

"You find this funny?" Belle whispered.

He lowered his mouth to her ear. "I was thinking we're like fish in a barrel."

"More like tuna in a tin can," she deadpanned.

Her comment added to his giddiness and his body bounced with a silent laugh. He pressed his lips together and tried to keep quiet. This was no time to be laughing, but he couldn't help it. It was his body's way of releasing the stress.

The gunfire ceased. Silence.

Had the gunman heard them? Was he reloading or moving toward them? Jonah stilled, and he held his breath, all mirth replaced with deadly attention.

The metal whomp of a car door flitted through the air. An engine revved to life and tires ate up loose gravel. Soon the approaching police sirens replaced the engine of the smaller vehicle. The gunman didn't plan to stick around, and for a split second Jonah considered chasing him. He rolled over onto his back, and instantly realized the plan wouldn't work.

His ribs screamed in protest. What was he thinking? They'd been in a rollover accident, and he was what? Going to chase this guy on foot? The mental image of himself limping after a car made him chuckle.

"What's with you?" Belle growled.

"I…I can't help it…" Laughter spilled out along with the remaining adrenaline. Belle giggled and the delicate sound only made things worse. The laughter caught like wildfire, each feeding the other one until they both couldn't quit.

Belle tucked her head into his side in an effort to muzzle herself, but her hot breath tickled. He squirmed and she took it as an invitation to do it again.

"Oh…ow!" He breathed. Each intake of breath burned his ribs, yet he couldn't stop. A tear trickled from the corner of his eye.

Over their laughing, he heard a dog barking and rustling foliage. The snap of a twig. A jingle.

In a flurry of fur and wagging tail, Oscar, Stella's search and rescue dog, wiggled his way into their hiding spot. The dog stuck his head between them; his entire body squirmed with excitement. He sniffed and nuzzled Belle's neck.

"Okay, okay!" she laughed. "You found us, Oscar. Good boy." She rubbed his ears.

The dog turned his attention to Jonah, snuffling and snorting. Oscar lifted his head and barked to alert his find.

"Over here!" Stella shouted. "Jonah, Belle? You guys in there?"

"We're here," he called back. "Under the back of the pickup."

"Good boy, Oscar! Come," Stella called.

Oscar gave Belle one last lick on her neck, then disappeared through the opening.

"You found them, Oscar. Yes, you did!" Stella praised her dog. "Belle? Jonah? Give me a rundown of your injuries."

Jonah glanced at Belle's stitches. Still intact. The scratch on her arm the only apparent injury. "Minor injuries. Belle has a small laceration on her forearm, but mostly bumps and bruises under here."

"If you could get this truck off us, I think we'll be okay," Belle said.

The rescue team moved into action with Riley the first to appear. "You guys ready to get out of there?"

"You have no idea," said Belle.

After draping a thick blanket over the broken glass, Riley helped them crawl through the rear window into the cab. They'd managed to get Jonah's door open and Deputy Lightfoot led them to Stella.

"Here, Abe." Stella gestured to a clearing near a tree

where she'd spread a clean blanket on the ground. "You guys sit here and let me take a look."

Jonah and Belle sat as instructed. Oscar lay nearby and gnawed a rubber dog toy.

"Sorry about your truck, Stella." The lame apology was all Jonah could muster. Exhaustion and a crushing headache clouded his thinking.

Stella looked up from her examination of Belle's arm and frowned. "Are you kidding? You two could have been killed. The truck can be replaced. You guys, not so much. Besides, that's an old farm truck, not my daily driver."

He offered a thin smile of gratitude and Belle squeezed his hand. Electricity zipped through his veins at her touch.

"At least we have matching head injuries," Belle chuckled.

Stella whirled on Jonah. "You hit your head? Where?"

"It's nothing. Other than a headache and muscle soreness, I'm fine."

"Oh, yeah just a little love tap on the noggin followed by a short nap," Belle said.

Jonah smiled. Belle had a way of lightening a serious moment, and even though he didn't want to be fawned over, he knew she was only trying to help.

Stella shone a penlight into each of his eyes while peppering him with questions. When she finished, she blew out a breath. "I think Belle's right. You might have a concussion. Let me check with Riley about getting you to the hospital."

Jonah looked at Belle who gave him a wan smile and mouthed the word *sorry*.

He gave her a soft shoulder bump.

Oscar finally gave up on his toy and laid his head in Belle's lap. She stroked his ears. "How smart you are, Oscar. You knew right where to find us."

"Pretty impressive actually. I know an agent with a human remains detection dog. It blows my mind to see him work."

"Human remains? You mean—?"

"Yep. They search and find…" His mind fumbled for a tactful word.

Her eyes went wide. "*Not* alive people?"

"Exactly."

Riley walked toward them, his phone pressed to his ear. He barked a few commands and disconnected the call. "A late model white sedan was reported stolen from the Lanes' place—that's the ranch about a quarter mile from Dr. McGee's. Our suspect abandoned it about two miles up the road. Big surprise. The road will be cleared sometime tonight." He turned to Stella and ran a hand over his bald head. "If you agree to keep them one more night, I'll come get them first thing in the morning and take them both to the hospital."

Stella chewed her lip for a moment. "I can agree to that, but only after I examine them at my office."

Jonah didn't want to agree to the hospital for himself. One step inside and someone might recognize his face. That spelled disaster. But he wasn't about to let Belle out of his sight. He could figure it out later. For now, he tried a Belle tactic and turned his words playful. "I guess we'll ride along. As long as you flash the sirens, Sheriff."

"Ha-ha, if I must." Riley's radio squawked and he turned his back to respond. Two short commands and he faced them again. "Listen, I need to clean up this mess. Stella, can you get them home? I'll check in later tonight."

Stella tucked a loose strand of hair behind her ear. "Sure, Linc. Feel free to stop by."

Jonah helped Belle get to her feet; Oscar followed suit. Tongue lolling out, the dog looked at Belle with admiration. Yeah, Jonah probably had a similar expression when he stared at Belle too.

Belle patted Oscar's side and turned her head to look uphill.

Jonah followed her gaze to the mangled guardrail where they'd left the road. Deep ruts cut into the rocky soil along the shoulder. A clear path appeared where the truck cut a swath through the trees, rolling over and crashing to its final resting spot against a boulder half the size of the truck. If the rock hadn't stopped them, they would have rolled another two hundred yards to the dirt road below.

A wave of fury rose deep in his chest at the sight of the truck. If he didn't know better, he'd wonder how anyone could have survived. He went to Belle and wrapped an arm around her, pulling her into a hug. She leaned into him, burying her face in his chest. He stroked her hair with one hand and held her with his other.

He flexed his jaw.

Whoever hunted Belle had no idea who they were dealing with, and the guy was in for a world of hurt the moment Jonah got his hands on him.

TWELVE

The next morning Belle forced herself to wake when she heard people moving throughout the house downstairs. The night had passed in a heavy, dreamless sleep. One she wanted to return to but knew she couldn't. By now the road would be cleared and Sheriff Riley promised to drive her to the hospital.

But then what?

She could go home, but…where was home? Still, she couldn't remember. Her address wouldn't be difficult to find, but it was her memories she really wanted. Would seeing a doctor even help? Doubtful, but it seemed the best course of action.

Belle drew herself into a sitting position with a wince. Every muscle in her body protested the movement. An aching soreness that stole her breath. Her ribs hurt. Her thighs hurt. Even her hair hurt. Was that possible? It must be, because her scalp burned when she ran her fingers through her curls. She delicately touched the stitches on her temple and the skin was cool. Not angry and hot. Not infected.

Reaching for the Bible on her bedside table resulted in a sharp pain in her side. Broken rib? She didn't bother to try again. Instead, she closed her eyes and said a prayer of thankfulness. Not only for their survival, but for the glimpse into her past.

Belinda.

The name she tried to utter when Jonah first found her.

Jonah. What was happening between them? She'd only known him a few days, and yet it seemed longer. The same familiarity she had the first day lingered and now grew into something else. Connectedness. The chemistry between them was undeniable, but something more than his physical appearance drew her in. Oh, she was attracted to him. No denying it. But their friendship deepened into a closeness she didn't want to abandon when they left Piney Village.

Could they explore their relationship in the face of the real world? His job was dangerous and required him to hide in a remote cabin for weeks, and hers...well she wasn't sure about her own career. Jonah spent his days deceiving bad men and manipulating them until they believed whatever he told them. Could she love a man who lived a lie? And what if they got married, had kids? Would they always be in hiding?

She closed her eyes and pinched the bridge of her nose. What was she thinking? Marriage and kids?

"Get a hold of yourself," she muttered.

One step at a time. A man's heart deviseth his way: but the LORD directeth his steps.

Was that a Bible verse she'd memorized? Another memory? She smiled at the Bible on her nightstand and decided to get out of bed and get moving. Today would be a big day.

Belle showered and dressed in the fresh clothes Stella left in the bathroom. The hot water did wonders for her stiff muscles, and she no longer worried about broken ribs. Bruised maybe, but not broken. The black-blue bruises on her neck looked worse, but they would fade in a few more days. She brushed her teeth and swallowed two ibuprofen before heading downstairs.

On the last stair, Belle heard the front door chime. Stella greeted Sheriff Riley as Belle rounded the corner.

"Morning, Sheriff," Belle said.

"Good morning. How you feelin' today?"

Belle followed Stella into the kitchen. "Sore, but I'm getting used to the feeling."

"Sorry, I know you've been through a lot the last few days," Riley said.

Jonah shook hands with Riley before turning to Belle. "Coffee might help. Let me get you a cup."

"Oh, thank you. My bones are aching for my caffeine fix."

"Sheriff? Coffee?" Jonah offered.

"Sure, but can we make it quick? The road is cleared, and we're set to drive you to the hospital. But first, we need to stop by the station." Riley eyed Jonah, communicating a silent message with his stare.

Jonah nodded and poured two cups. "Belle, how did you sleep?"

"Like a log. How are you feeling this morning?"

"A little sore," he said, handing them their mugs. "And your memory? Did everything come flooding back yet?"

"Hah, very funny." She rolled her eyes and took a slow sip of her coffee. Why would Riley want to speak to Jonah at the station? Did he know something about the attacker he wasn't ready to share with her?

After a light breakfast and one more cup of coffee, she climbed into the backseat of Riley's SUV with Jonah. On the quiet drive to town, Belle stared out the window and watched the scenery slip by. A family of deer and two fawns grazed near the lake. Beautiful. Peaceful. She released a soft sigh. This wasn't home, but it sure felt like it.

She turned to Jonah and caught him staring at her, the corners of his mouth turned up in a smile. The man sure was handsome. No denying it. As if on its own, her hand reached for his. They entwined their fingers without a word and Jonah didn't release her hand until Riley parked in front of the station.

They followed Riley inside and Annie paused her reading.

"Good to see you again," she said. "Sorry about all the trouble lately. Sheriff, there's a…um…visitor waiting for you in the conference room."

"Thanks, can you let him know I'll be right there?"

Without a word, Annie scurried down the hall and around the corner.

"Belle, if you'll excuse us. Jonah and I need to have a private meeting. We have coffee. Just ask Annie and she'll fix you up with anything you need."

"Do you think I could use a computer? I'd like to read more about myself online if that's possible. Maybe it will spark memories."

"Sure, you take that desk right there." He pointed to the one behind Annie's. "I'll let her know it's okay."

Jonah took Belle's hand and stroked her fingers with his thumb. "I'll be right in there if you need anything. Don't go anywhere until I get back, okay?"

Belle grinned. "Where would I go?"

He lifted her hand to his lips and kissed it. Heat rushed to her cheeks, and she averted her eyes to her feet. When he turned to go, she willed her racing heart to calm. He was leaving the room, not leaving the earth.

She waited until he disappeared down the hall, then sat at the computer and wiggled the mouse to bring the screen to life. A search engine page waited. The name Dr. McGee found still seemed foreign to her, but she typed *Dr. Belinda Lewis* and hit Enter.

The first page of results appeared, and she scrolled, glancing at the titles. Various articles she'd published in the National Library of Medicine displayed. Several included her research partner Dr. Robert Winn. Belle did a similar search, but images only. She studied her face in the photos. Yep, it was her all right. Unless she had a twin sister she never knew about.

Annie sat at her desk and swiveled her chair toward Belle. "Is that you?" she asked. "Did your memory return?"

"The photo is me, yes. And my memory…well it's taking its sweet time about coming back, but it *is* coming back."

"That's wonderful. I'd hate to forget my life. The good and the bad, if you know what I mean." She wiggled her ring finger at Belle, displaying the white line where a wedding band used to be. "He was an abusive drunk, but I still loved him."

Belle didn't know how to respond. The idea of a man hitting Annie made her stomach twist. Attacked by a stranger was one thing, but attacked by someone you loved…that was a whole other type of torture. Annie deserved better.

Belle's eyes drifted back to the computer, and she stared at the photo of Robert Winn. His arm around her shoulders, grinning ear to ear. Suddenly she remembered him. She thought she loved him, and he'd betrayed her. A weight settled in her chest making it difficult to breathe.

She sprang from the chair. "I need some air."

Before Annie could respond, she pushed her way through the front door. Outside, she walked to the passenger side of the sheriff's SUV, out of Annie's view through the window.

She leaned over, hands on her knees, and gasped for breath. The burning sensation spread throughout her aching ribs and deep into her stomach. Her head began to spin. If she didn't slow her breathing, she'd hyperventilate and pass out.

Using her index finger, she pressed one nostril closed and flattened her lips to force herself to breathe from the other nostril. Somehow, she knew this method of restricting oxygen flow helped in the past. Soon, her pulse slowed, and each breath came easier.

A shadow moved in the corner of her eye. Before she could turn, a sharp pain pricked her neck. She crumpled to the ground and her vision faded to black.

Seeing Special Agent in Charge Chase Bishop standing in the interview room threw Jonah for a loop. He was the last person Jonah expected to see, but of course Chase wanted to debrief him and in-person interviews always trumped a phone interview. But this time, Jonah didn't need to worry about suppressing microexpressions or hiding his deception—something he was exceptionally good at after working undercover for years. Chase wasn't here to catch him out. He wanted a complete report, and that was what Jonah spent twenty minutes giving him.

When he'd finished, Chase reached over and clicked off his recording device. He laced his fingers behind his head and leaned back. "Wow. You really don't know what it means to lay low, do you?"

Riley and Jonah both chuckled. "They've been keeping me on my toes, that's for sure," Riley said.

"You should know we've invited Sheriff Riley into the joint task force for the Trailside Strangler. Whether that's who is behind all the attacks or not, we can use his help with the investigation. And…" Chase dropped his hands and let them rest on the thick file folder in front of him.

The silence stretched but Jonah waited it out. This wasn't drama; Chase was collecting his thoughts. Preparing for the best way to deliver a devastating blow.

He opened the file folder and withdrew a photograph. He slid it across the table to Jonah. "You've seen this photo. It's the one the facial recognition software matched to you. Looks like you, right?"

Jonah flicked his gaze to Riley, who sat with his arms folded across his broad chest.

"Yeah, kinda. He looks like me, but it's not me and you know it. Couldn't be me." He flicked the photograph away. "You have surveillance coming out of your ears proving I was undercover in Rico's warehouse."

"We know it's not you," Chase said. "But take a closer look at the photo. He *looks* like you, doesn't he?"

Jonah examined the photo. The guy did look similar.

"Jonah, we unsealed your adoption records. The original birth record was marked as a multiple birth. This man…" He gestured to the photo. "He's your identical twin brother."

"Twin…brother." He repeated the words, but they didn't register. Twin? How could he have a twin and not know it?

"His name is Malachi Pry. We dug up an old police report your father completed. When you were three years old, he found you and Malachi at a murder-suicide scene. Your biological mother's murder. Your biological father strangled her to death, then hanged himself. A caseworker took you and Malachi from the scene to the ER where your adoptive parents agreed to take you home."

"Wait, both of us? My parents *knew* I had a twin?"

Chase nodded. "They agreed after such trauma you both needed a loving home. They proceeded with the adoption paperwork immediately."

Things weren't making sense. He'd just learned he was adopted and now Chase was saying his parents knew about his twin brother and never told him? "What happened? Did they adopt Malachi?"

"I read through about ten binders of handwritten case notes left by your social worker. During the waiting period for adoption, your parents reported several incidents of Malachi wrapping things around his neck." Chase paused and locked his eyes on to Jonah's. "The team thought it best to separate you temporarily and get Malachi the help he needed."

"Temporarily? No, I never knew about this…this… Malachi Pry! I never even knew I'd been adopted." Jonah ran his hands through his hair. Pressure built in his chest, and he did a ten count to regain control. "Keep going—I want to hear all of it."

"You had a couple of visits, but they seemed to make Malachi upset. The counselors thought your presence only retraumatized him, so they stopped the visits. Your adoption moved forward. Malachi's didn't. He bounced from foster home to foster home with behavioral issues that grew worse as he got older. Even after several long stints in a psychiatric hospital and spending his childhood in therapy, Malachi never improved."

"What's his diagnosis?" Riley asked.

"The usual. Off-the-charts intelligence. Depression, anxiety, reactive attachment disorder. There are others in here." He tapped the folder. "You can see why they kept you apart all these years."

Jonah swallowed hard. "You're saying my twin brother

grew up to become a serial killer because he witnessed our father kill our mother and then himself?"

"That's the profiler's theory."

"What's the theory about Jonah then? He saw the same thing." Riley gestured at Jonah. "He's on the right side of the law."

"No one knows how these things work." Chase sighed.

Jonah needed more information. Chase had just shattered Jonah's reality. It would take time to make sense of it all. The more facts he could obtain now, the better he could process things later.

"What happened to him? I mean, after foster care," Jonah said.

"Hang on—let's backtrack for a minute," Chase said. "You inherited the cabin and land when your mother passed away, correct?"

"That's right."

Chase and Riley exchanged a knowing look.

"The land was owned by your biological parents, Jonah," Riley said. "It's where their murder happened all those years ago. The property was purchased by your adoptive parents, and they left it to you."

Jonah stared blankly at the conference table. His mind working to piece together the details.

"The profilers believe leaving his victims nearby was his strange way of getting your attention," Chase said.

Riley studied the photo. "I guess that explains why he kidnapped victims from other areas and left their bodies around here. He wanted them closer to *home*." He slid the photo toward Chase.

"So, my twin brother, this…this…Malachi Pry. He's the Trailside Strangler?"

Chase nodded. "That's our theory."

"And what? He decided to hunt victims closer to my

cabin and Belle was hiking in the wrong place at the wrong time?"

"Not exactly." Chase pushed a piece of paper to Jonah.

He snatched it and read the eyewitness report of the woman who interrupted the Trailside Strangler and helped his victim escape. Right there in black-and-white, the name jumped off the page.

Dr. Belinda Lewis.

His mouth went dry.

"Dr. Lewis—Belle as you call her—was conducting field research at an alpine lake about ten miles from here when she heard a woman scream. She ran to help and had the presence of mind to snap a photo of the attacker when he was scared off." Chase tapped the photograph on the table. "Malachi released the young woman and escaped on foot. It fit the MO and the case agents interviewed the witness."

"Belle…" Jonah whispered.

"Because of her courage and quick thinking, we finally have a suspect."

"Malachi isn't hunting Belle because she escaped him in the woods," Jonah said softly. "He's hunting her because she's the witness to his kidnapping."

"We haven't concluded the investigation," Chase said. "We need to conduct a proper interview of you both."

Jonah sat back and stared at the table blankly, unsure how to process the information. His life was forever changed from one conversation. He had a brother. A twin. And if he was the Trailside Strangler then Belle was still in danger.

"So, what are the next steps? I must protect Belle until Malachi is arrested."

Chase cleared his throat and tucked the papers back into his file. "I'll drive you and Belle to the hospital. Special Agent Zeke Harrison will meet us there. He'll be on security. I have the US Marshals on standby if we need to move her to WITSEC."

Jonah nodded. "I know Zeke—he's a good guy. And I agree, Belle's safety is priority. I think we should get her to the hospital and under protection before anything else can happen."

The men stood to leave.

"I need to stop by my office and return a call real quick," Riley said.

Before Jonah could leave the interview room, Chase caught him by the arm. "Watch how close you get to this woman, Jonah. She's our only eyewitness in this serial killer case and you're too close to this. We can't risk her testimony being thrown out because you stuck your nose into an investigation where your twin brother is the main suspect. You're playing with fire, and I personally don't want to watch your career go up in flames." He released Jonah's arm and brushed past on his way out.

Jonah rubbed the back of his neck and drew in a deep breath. He wanted to argue, but Chase wasn't wrong. This whole thing could blow up in his face and worse, put more innocent lives at risk. It was always that way. His job or a personal life, but he couldn't have both. It was a difficult lesson he learned the hard way on the night he lost his college sweetheart, Amy.

But this wasn't about Amy; it was about Belle. With the road clear, they could get Belle to the hospital and have her in protective custody by noon. Saying goodbye wouldn't be easy, but he would have to let her go and now was as good a time as any…even if his heart didn't agree.

He kicked a rolling chair and sent it spinning into the table. With a forceful smack, he hit the light switch on his way out of the room.

He didn't see Belle in the bullpen. She wasn't at the computer or standing with Chase and Riley. She wasn't anywhere in the small office. "Annie, where's Belle?"

"Oh, she said she needed some air and stepped right outside." She gestured to the window. "I could see her feet right— Wait, where'd she go?"

"How long has she been outside?" Riley asked.

"Uh, I think twenty…maybe thirty minutes," Annie guessed.

Jonah broke into a sprint and slammed the door with both hands, shoving his way outside. His head swiveled in both directions, searching the street. No sign of Belle anywhere.

"I'll check the alley this way," Riley said. "Chase, you go that way. Jonah, stay right here in case she comes back."

The two men ran in opposite directions. Jonah's muscles twitched. No way could he stand here with his hands in his pockets. He had to do something. With a cupped hand, he peeked through the windows of the sheriff's SUV. Nothing. He squatted, then lowered himself to his stomach to check underneath the vehicle. A black spot on the ground caught his eye. It wasn't there when he'd hopped out of the vehicle earlier. He pulled himself to his feet and ran around the SUV and knelt.

With his index finger, he dabbed the wet spot and rubbed it between his finger and thumb. The sight of the thick, sticky liquid on his fingertips catapulted his heart rate.

"What's that?" Riley asked.

Jonah looked over his shoulder, then to his fingers. "It's blood."

THIRTEEN

"Once again, she tried to show you up!" The man screeched the last word. "And it's working. Ohhhh iiiit's working."

The frenzied voice jarred Belle awake, and she cracked an eyelid. Bright sunshine stabbed her vision and she squinted, straining to open her eyes. Her eyelids fluttered until she could focus, but what she saw didn't make sense. Dirt. Mere feet from her face, bootheels traipsed over the rocky mountain terrain. Someone carried her over their shoulder.

Her eyelids drooped. Groggy. So groggy. She tried to lift her arms, but their weight threatened to drag her back into unconsciousness. With each step the man took, her body shifted.

"She thinks she's smarter than you," he grumbled. "She'll tell the world what you did and expose you to everyone."

Her blood ran cold at his words and the mind fog evaporated. That wasn't the man who'd spoken before. Was there *two* of them?

Every instinct propelled her to fight. Claw her way out of this man's grasp and bolt. But her body wouldn't cooperate. She turned her head, hoping to glimpse the second kidnapper. A glint of metal caught her eye. The barrel of a rifle rested on his opposite shoulder. Striking right now wouldn't work. Even if she managed to break free, she wouldn't take more than a few steps before one of them shot her dead. No, she'd only have one chance to escape alive and patience was the only weapon she wielded. She'd quashed her attacker's plans before, and she could do it again—if she waited for the right moment.

A plan formulated. Pretend to be unconscious so they let their guard down. Turned their backs on her or left a weapon unattended. One mistake and a few seconds was all she needed.

She forced herself to relax and let her arms go limp. Listening and memorizing every detail of her surroundings including the scents of sweat, pine needles and earth. From her limited view, everything looked the same. Trees, trees and more trees with the occasional rock or fallen limb to break the pattern. No landmarks she could identify.

The warm sun tingled her skin. It was still daylight, but how long had she been unconscious? Minutes? Hours? No telling. He could've thrown her in a car and driven to Utah for all she knew. It didn't matter. Even if she couldn't escape, Jonah would come for her. Deep down in her gut she knew he'd never stop searching until he found her.

The man slowed his pace and picked his way down a hill, zigzagging his way around rocks and bushes. At the bottom, he turned and carried her past an arched rock wall made of hand-stacked stones. He opened the dilapidated door and a blast of cool, musty air hit her face. A high-pitched screech emanated from the corroded hinges. No way could she sneak out without someone hearing.

The narrow doorway required him to twist and maneuver his way through the opening. A strand of her hair caught on the door and pinched her scalp. She clenched her teeth until the wave of pain passed. He walked ten paces and turned around. With a shrug of his shoulders, he dumped her onto the smooth dirt floor.

An involuntary grunt slipped out before she could stop it. The man whirled around and nudged her stomach with his boot. She mumbled a groan and curled into a fetal position. He lingered, but she remained motionless and silently prayed he'd believe her feigned sleep.

The man walked away, and she opened her eyes the tiniest slit. Through her eyelashes, she saw the man's brown hiking boots. No one else was in the room.

The man walked to the door then spun on his heel and retraced his steps. She counted. Ten to the door, ten back. Spin and repeat. He drifted back and forth in this manner, muttering. The words too quiet and unintelligible to make sense. Was he on a phone?

Each time he turned away, she opened her eyes and studied the room. Horizontal logs lined the walls of the room with some placed vertically to support the wooden braces for the roof. Her cheek rested on a loosely packed dirt floor.

Her stomach sank. She knew what the room was. He'd hidden her in an old root cellar built into the hillside. Hundreds of cellars like this one dotted the mountains of Colorado. Sometimes several on one homestead. Insulated by layers of logs, rock, soil and whatever wild plants grew, her screams would go unnoticed.

"I told you," the man screamed. "You can't kill her until she gives me *all* the research!"

Belle closed her eyes and waited while he circled back and paced the ten steps to stand near her. So close she could smell the stench of sweat.

When he turned his back, she lifted her head for a

better look. The man didn't wear hunting camouflage as she expected. He wore a navy T-shirt and navy cargo pants. A bulge in his lower back told her he had a pistol tucked in his waistband, and the rifle rested on his shoulder. She didn't see a phone, but maybe he had one of those wireless earpieces.

A prick of an idea kicked her thoughts into overdrive.

Malachi Pry. Jonah's gut twisted and crawled like a pit of snakes. How could his own brother, his only living blood relative, be the killer tracking Belle? And worse, a serial murderer.

Jonah examined his hands. Were they the same hands Malachi wrapped around the thin necks of his prey?

He dropped his hands and shoved them into his pockets. He might be Malachi's twin physically, but he didn't have the same dead heart as his brother. Malachi's dark heart prowled the night for unsuspecting victims. Jonah's heart refused to harm the innocent and he vowed to protect, not to kill. It was Malachi's cold indifference that slaughtered women and dumped their bodies all over the Rocky Mountain National Park.

Stella's truck came to a sliding halt on the asphalt and parked behind the sheriff's SUV. Riley stepped off the sidewalk where he'd been waiting with Jonah, Deputy Lightfoot and the young park ranger Riley had introduced as Talia King. Two other rangers with excellent tracking skills had headed out on horseback less than five minutes earlier. Chase hung back at the sheriff's office to coordinate an air search.

Jonah pushed the thought of Malachi's killing rituals aside and half jogged to meet Stella. He forced himself to forget about his own issues and focus on finding Belle.

Riley rushed to Stella's truck and opened the door.

"Thanks for bringing Oscar so quickly," he said. "We sure can use his help finding Belle."

"Of course," Stella breathed. She hopped down and hurried to the back door and released Oscar. The dog wore an orange vest with reflective stripes and the words Search Dog in bold letters along his side. Stella wore her own orange vest with the words K9 Search and Rescue printed on the back. She clipped a leash to Oscar's harness.

Stella gave Jonah a firm hug. "Don't worry. We'll get her back."

"I just hope it's not too late," Jonah said.

Stella squeezed his arm. "Don't hope. *Pray.*" She walked to the blood spot and squatted beside it. "Are you sure this is Belle's blood? Could it belong to an animal or someone else?"

"Annie said that's where she saw Belle standing last, but we're not one hundred percent sure it's Belle's blood," Riley said.

"We can't risk sending Oscar off on the wrong scent." Stella stood and pulled a clear zippered bag from her vest pocket. "Good thing I brought a backup."

"What is that?" Talia asked.

"It's Belle's pillowcase. I grabbed it on the way out, just in case. Ready when you are, Linc."

"Okay, people. Keep your radios on and check in every ten minutes. Talia, can you get that utility terrain vehicle?"

"You mean the UTV with the medical rescue kit?" Talia asked.

"Yes, that. Can you take Abe and prepare for an extraction?"

"Of course."

"Thanks. The rest of us are on foot with Oscar. Listen for the mounted rangers and let's try not to trample any evidence. The FBI search and rescue team is on standby. Any questions?"

Jonah's blood pressure continued to climb with every second they stood around and chatted instead of finding Belle. "Can we get going? No telling how far he's gotten by now and we're standing here wasting time."

The remark came out harsh and Jonah regretted it as soon as the words left his mouth. Spending five minutes to organize now would save hours of time later and he knew it. That usual sense of calm under pressure he normally possessed in these situations seemed to have vanished with Belle, and it rattled him.

Riley let the comment slide. "Let's move out. Stella, you're in the lead."

Stella caught Jonah's attention and mouthed the word *pray*.

The idea of praying only to have the same outcome as his previous prayers caused a lump to lodge in his throat and he wasn't sure he could speak if he tried. Prayer didn't work for him. He'd prayed for his father and God let him die. He'd prayed for his mother and God let her die. If he prayed to find Belle alive, would God let her die too?

Stella knelt beside her dog. "Okay, Oscar. You ready to work?"

The dog wagged his tail, and Stella unzipped the bag containing Belle's pillowcase and opened it. Oscar stuck his nose inside and sniffed the contents with interest.

"Oscar, find Belle."

The dog withdrew his blocky head, and his body went rigid. His long brown tail stopped swaying and stiffened. He twitched his nose and circled. The muscular dog shot off like a rocket and Jonah didn't hesitate to follow.

He broke into a sprint. They followed Oscar past the

sheriff's office and around the corner onto the narrow road leading beside the building. Good thing the dog was on a twenty-foot lead because Jonah couldn't keep pace. Stella commanded the dog to Wait at the end of the road, though Oscar paused as if he knew he shouldn't cross the road on his own.

Oscar led them to a dirt path heading into the forest and turned to look at them as if to say, *C'mon, she went this way.*

"Good boy, Oscar. Keep going. Find Belle," Stella encouraged.

The dog trotted into the forest following the scent along a dirt trail. Stella stayed behind Oscar, occasionally dropping his leash to allow him to maneuver around a tree before scooping it up again.

Jonah followed Stella's lead although he wanted to dash out ahead of everyone and stick close to Oscar. Encourage the dog to go faster. But this was Stella's expertise. As a team, they'd done this countless times and she knew how her dog worked. Best to let her do her thing with Oscar.

The muddy trail led them east, away from the village and deeper into the surrounding wilderness. They wove in and out between towering aspens and pines that mercifully provided much-needed shade from the harsh sun. Twigs snagged his clothes, and he was glad he'd worn long sleeves despite the heat.

"How do we know we're even going the right way?" Jonah asked. "What if Oscar is on the wrong scent?"

"He's trained to stay on scent until he loses it. Don't worry—he'll let me know if he does."

"I've seen that dog track over a thousand acres," Riley said. "He almost always finds his mark."

"And the times he didn't?"

Jonah watched Stella's shoulders rise and fall. Even from behind he knew she'd sighed. "Right now, Oscar has a good scent. Let's focus on following him and watching for anything Belle or her kidnapper may have dropped."

They trudged on, winding around rocks and tall trees with smooth white trunks. Twice Jonah caught his toe on a root jutting out of the ground and he stumbled.

Without turning around, Stella chastised him. "Your instincts tell you to look around for a glimpse of Belle, but it's better to keep your gaze low and watch your step."

"Yeah, I see that," Jonah muttered.

They walked in silence, one behind the other until Riley's radio keyed up. Abe and Talia with a status check. Riley updated their location, and said Oscar was tracking on scent and they should continue to stand by. The horseback trackers said they'd followed a track south but ended up startling a group of hikers. Riley suggested the trackers head back and remain on standby as well.

Listening to Riley issuing commands chafed Jonah's ego. As an FBI agent, he should have a role in the operation other than coming along for the ride. Of course, he remained on sabbatical, and Chase made it clear he wanted Jonah to keep his agent status under wraps. At least they let him keep his sidearm and participate in the search.

As he watched his step and navigated another gnarled tree root, he bumped into Stella, not realizing she'd stopped. "Oof, sorry."

He glanced over to see Oscar about ten feet away, waiting patiently atop a flat boulder overlooking the valley below.

"What's wrong? Why did he stop?"

"Nothing is wrong. He's waiting for permission to go down that hill in case it isn't safe. Good boy, Oscar. Let's find Belle."

Oscar hopped off the rock and picked his way through the brush. Jonah was no expert tracker, but even he could see areas of broken and flattened foliage.

With each step his uneasiness grew. Malachi had dragged Belle through this wide-open field without anyone noticing. Just like he'd kidnapped Belle right out from under his nose without a single witness.

Jonah snatched a long blade of grass and wrapped it around his finger until red lines appeared. He unwrapped it and repeated the process.

Some FBI agent he turned out to be. How could he not know about his own twin brother? Didn't twins have some unexplainable connection? His parents should have told him about Malachi, but he supposed it was easier to avoid the painful past than to face the truth.

But look where that landed him. Where it landed Belle. A killer for a brother and biological parents he never had the opportunity to grieve. He'd lost Amy and two sets of parents in one lifetime. Was he about to lose Belle too?

Please, God, no. Not Belle. She loves You and even after forgetting her entire life, she never forgot You. Never gave up on You. Please don't give up on her.

It wasn't a prayer, but rather a one-sided conversation with God. His heart wasn't ready to pray exactly, but what harm could it do to talk to God?

A sharp bark from Oscar caused Jonah to jerk to attention. Ahead, the dog paced the bank of a stream with his nose on the ground.

Jonah raced to where Oscar waited. "What's he doing? Did he find her?"

Stella and Riley exchanged a look.

"What? What is it?" Jonah's voice rose to near yelling.

A dark cloud fell over Stella's face. "I'm sorry, Jonah. He's lost the scent."

FOURTEEN

Belle dropped her head and closed her eyes before the kidnapper turned and walked back toward her, mumbling to himself. Or was he mumbling to the person on the other end of the phone? It didn't matter. With only one man to deal with, Belle had a chance. It was a risk, but she had to take it. Think logically. Be patient. Catch him off guard.

Each time he paced away, she quietly groped the ground around her for something to use as a weapon. Her fingers found something cool and hard near her knee and she wrapped her hand around a rock. When she realized the size was too small to do any damage, the edges too smooth, her heart plummeted. She slipped the rock into her pocket and continued to feel around for something, anything else.

"I will get that research if it's the last thing I do!" The man screamed the words and stomped the remaining three steps to the cellar door. He yanked it open, and sunlight poured in.

Belle blinked and tried to focus on the man's face, but the door cast a shadow over him. He stormed outside and the door screeched shut behind him. In an instant, Belle sat up and frantically searched for a weapon.

Outside, the man continued to shout about research.

She had no idea what he was talking about, and she didn't plan to stick around to find out. One way or another, she had to escape.

She peeked at the door. Through the warped slats, she saw him moving back and forth. A rock the size of her hand near the door caught her eye. Could she get to it before he came back inside? It was her only chance and she had to try.

She was about to stand when she heard the squeak of the rusty doorknob. Quickly she resumed her position on the floor and pretended to be unconscious. The man flung the door closed behind him and stormed across the room. Her blood froze as he towered over her. She could hear his panting breath and sense his fury.

With him standing over her and armed with two guns, Belle was desperately vulnerable. There was nowhere to go if he pulled his pistol and took aim. Her heart thundered so hard in her chest she was sure he could hear it.

Using the tip of his boot he poked her stomach. "You awake? You need to tell me where it is." His voice, deeper and less frantic than earlier, seemed familiar. "I know you're hiding it. I saw your notebook at work the other day."

At work? This man knew her. He drove his boot into her side and rolled her onto her back. She groaned and lolled her head, but kept her eyes closed.

His knees cracked as he lowered himself to squat beside her. "You discovered a new genus of algae, didn't you? Don't deny it. I read your notes," his husky voice lowered to a whisper. "The new eukaryotic algae is the organic sunscreen the world has been waiting for. You'll be rich and famous. And you're trying to keep it to yourself. You make me sick!"

He stood and spat in her face. She remained motionless despite the compulsion to flinch and wipe away his disgusting saliva. The man laughed and wheeled back toward the door.

A pulse of red danced behind her eyelids. There was something about the man she recognized. Surely she knew him, but she still couldn't remember. An impulse overwhelmed her. Without thinking, she sprang to her feet and lunged for him. In a flash, she wrenched the gun from his waistband and pointed it at his head. She stepped back, adding distance between them.

"Drop the rifle," she said. "Slowly."

With one thumb he lifted the strap of the rifle off his shoulder and let the gun fall to the ground.

"Kick it to me."

He didn't move.

"Now!" She pulled the slide back and chambered a bullet. Her thumb found the safety and clicked it off.

With the heel of his boot, he shoved the rifle in her direction. She stretched her leg until her foot found the stock and dragged it toward her.

"Both hands up and turn around."

His hands slowly rose, and he faced her.

Deep in her gut, recognition flared. She knew him.

Memories of her past came flooding back and she realized she held a gun on Dr. Robert Winn.

"You…" she said. "All this time it was you?"

"Let's cut the pretense, shall we? You've been holding out on me, Belinda."

The organic sunscreen research. He was right; she was holding out on him. Instead of growing the algae in the lab, she conducted her experiments in nature. Hiked up to Eagle Lake each week to retrieve samples and make notes alone so he couldn't steal her work. The same lake where she'd been attacked.

"You stole my work once, Robert. You think I'd let you steal it again?"

"Belinda," he crooned. "That was a misunderstanding. The university made a mistake."

"Then why did you accept the awards, the grant money? You gave yourself a big fat salary and took all the credit." She hated how her voice shook.

Memories of the entire situation bubbled up as if it happened moments ago instead of over a year ago. Memories of how he'd flirted and charmed his way into her heart. Took her to dinner and stayed at the lab late into the night. It was all an act.

A hot tear escaped at his duplicity. "I gave you everything and you betrayed me."

"You're misreading the situation, Belinda." He took a half step toward her.

"Stop saying my name," she yelled. "You don't know me, and we are certainly not friends."

"We are friends. We were more than friends, remember?" Another half step.

"Don't come any closer or I'll shoot you right here."

Robert's face twisted and contorted. A change flashed behind his eyes. His hands rose to cover his ears and he frantically shook his head like he was trying to block out some noise Belle couldn't hear.

"No! Nooooo! Don't hurt her," he wailed. The frenzied voice she'd heard earlier returned. Softer and higher-pitched. Almost child-like. With his hands still over his ears, he shuffled backward. "You—You can't… Leave… Leave her… Leave her alone!"

Belle gaped. The man was losing it. Either that or it was some sort of trick to get her to put the gun down. She gripped her hand tighter around the pistol. She'd come too far to lose her only chance at getting out of here alive. One wrong move and she wouldn't hesitate to pull the trigger.

Robert's breathing accelerated into audible panting through his teeth that made a shh-shh-shh sound each time he sucked in air. He dropped his hands from his ears and began pacing the room again. This time, instead of pacing the length of the space he went side to side only managing a few steps before he met the wall and was forced to turn. Lost in his own thoughts, he fixed his eyes on the floor and rambled to himself.

She tracked him with the gun. Every nerve crackled with energy. Something was odd about his behavior. He appeared disturbed and that made him dangerous. Heart pounding, she adjusted her stance and prepared to shoot if he attacked.

"Robert, stop."

He came to an abrupt halt. His gaze met hers and he studied her with a quizzical look. "I'm not Robert," he said. "I'm Bobby."

After several minutes of patrolling the bank, Oscar still hadn't picked up Belle's scent anywhere along the edge of the water. Stella had decided they should cross the shallow stream and try something she called casting to help Oscar find the trail again. Now Stella walked the dog back and forth in an ever-growing semicircle, moving up and down the bank hoping he'd find Belle's scent. It was clear from Oscar's body language he hadn't found the trail. Muscles loose, the dog trotted along the bank with his tail swaying.

Jonah waited nearby with Riley, their pants soaked up to their knees from wading across the frigid water. On any other day, listening to the clear water rush over the smooth boulders would bring Jonah peace, but in this moment the cacophony aggravated his already tight nerves.

He thrust a hand into his hair and raked it back. Stella and Oscar were moving farther and farther away. "He's not finding it," Jonah said. "What do we do?"

Riley glanced at his watch. "It's only been ten minutes. Give him another five and if we don't have it, I'll call the standby team."

A low growl escaped with Jonah's forceful exhale.

"Look, I know it's difficult to stand here feeling like we're doing nothing, but it's a process, not an exact science. We make our plans, and we follow procedure for a good reason. You should understand it better than most."

Jonah sucked in a breath and pushed it out through his nostrils. "You're right—I'm sorry. I trust you and Stella… and Oscar. I guess the last few days I'm feeling less like an agent and more like a helpless victim."

"Yeah, been there." Riley folded his arms over his broad chest and looked past Jonah toward the mountains. "I lost someone in these mountains. It ain't easy and—"

Whining from Oscar interrupted Riley and they turned to see the dog two hundred yards upstream. Body rigid and tail stiff, the dog was back on scent.

Stella followed her dog and Jonah fought the impulse to flat-out run to Stella and stay on her heels. Maybe even kiss Oscar right on his brilliant nose. Instead, he took his cue from Riley and trekked through the field to meet Stella in silence.

Riley had been about to tell Jonah something important when Oscar cut him off. He itched for Riley to continue. The distraction would take his mind off the heaviness of their present situation. Desiring Riley to talk about his own pain to alleviate Jonah's anxiety seemed selfish, so he let it drop.

Oscar trotted along the bank for almost a quarter mile before he veered off. The ground sloped into a gentle elevation gain without a trail in sight. The dog led them to a new forest of conifers and worked his way through the thick growth. This area appeared untouched by hikers with massive branches forcing them to duck or climb over. Did a kidnapper really force Belle through here?

The climb grew arduous, and Jonah's lungs began to burn, demanding more oxygen. Oscar didn't seem to notice. Intent on pursuing Belle's trail, he drove them up the mountainside. Stella let his leash out the full twenty feet, allowing Oscar to gain some distance. They labored behind him without wasting precious breath on speaking.

When they finally broke through the dense trees and into an open area, Stella called to Oscar and asked him to wait. "Let's take a few minutes," she breathed.

Jonah withdrew the water bottle out of his back pocket and took a long pull while taking in the view. From their resting spot he admired how the foothills folded over each other. Fluffy white clouds lingered a hair above the ridge line. Deep in the valley, a river snaked around and met the tributary they'd crossed earlier, now a mere speck of icy blue in a sea of greenery.

They'd covered a surprising amount of terrain in a short amount of time. No wonder he was hot and out of breath. He drained his water down to the last sip, which he decided to keep in reserve.

Riley called in their position.

Talia's voice crackled over the radio. "I know that area. There are a few old homesteads nearby. They're abandoned now, but the suspect could have Belle stashed in one."

Riley worked his jaw for a moment. "Oscar has her scent, so we'll continue on foot. Everyone else, move into the area and clear every building in the vicinity. Use extreme caution. Suspect is considered armed and dangerous."

Riley locked eyes with Jonah. They were close to finding Belle, but in what condition? Had Malachi already strangled her to death and left her body in the woods for them to find? Could Oscar find Belle if she was dead? He didn't want to know.

As if reading his mind, Stella gave him a thin smile. "One way or another, we'll find her, Jonah."

He couldn't risk speaking and simply nodded.

"Oscar, find Belle," Stella commanded.

Without missing a beat, the dog went back to work. His nose twitched and he wove in a zigzagging motion tracing something Stella called a scent cone. In minutes, Jonah could see a visible change in Oscar. He moved faster, stretching his leash to the limit. Muscles taut and mind focused on his task.

They were close. Very close.

FIFTEEN

Belle clutched the pistol with a steady grip and pointed it at the kidnapper on the floor. She'd maneuvered him to the back of the cellar and forced him to sit in the same spot where he had dumped her earlier.

Getting him into the position wasn't easy. His agitation was off the charts, and she couldn't get him to listen. It took her shouting at the top of her lungs to break through his muttering and gain his attention. They slowly circled each other until she had him at the back of the cellar.

With the gun pointed at him, she could've backed away and made her escape. She *should* have, but something stopped her from leaving. Instead of bolting out the door, she stood rooted in place, trying to wrap her mind around the outrageousness of it all.

When she began a relationship with Dr. Robert Winn, it didn't take long to realize something was off. His personality changed drastically from day to day. It was clear he struggled with depression and bursts of anger that affected his work and his relationships. But multiple personalities? She never would've guessed it.

So far, she'd only met two of his identities, but each knew about the other. Maybe even worked together. Were his personalities merging?

"Tell me your name," she demanded.

"I already told you, I'm Bobby." He didn't bother to look at her and continued to pick at the skin around his fingernails. Unconcerned about the gun she held on him.

He had told her. She'd questioned him for almost half an hour already, but his answers all sounded like delusion. Like some big trick he was trying to play.

"You're not Bobby—you're Robert. Dr. Robert Winn, my—"

"NO! I already told you, Robert isn't in charge right now. He wants to kill you, and I won't let him."

She swallowed the rising acid in her throat. "Why… Why does Robert want to kill me?"

Bobby waved a dismissive hand. "How many times do I have to explain it? I'm starting to think he's right about you. Maybe you're not as smart as you think you are."

"Please, Bobby. I want to hear it again. One more time?" Being nice to the man who'd nearly killed her and Jonah multiple times made her skin crawl.

"Fiiine… I'll tell you again. Then we can head to your research."

"I… I'll try. I need a map to help me locate it. Maybe a phone? We can call someone to give us a ride."

He wagged his index finger. "Nice try, Belinda. You know the way and we can find it together. We don't need anyone else."

Earlier when she'd mentioned Jonah, Bobby had flown into a rage. He held some perceived ownership over her and didn't like seeing her with Jonah. She could tell Robert used Bobby's jealousy to take control.

"Okay, it will be just us," she placated him. She wanted to keep talking to Bobby. "Now, tell me why Robert wants to kill me."

"Oh, you know Robert…he's always overreacting. You said you planned to file a complaint for stealing your research. He got the bright idea to kill you and make it look like that serial killer did it, but I told him to wait until I found your algae project. But he's soooo impulsive. He's been following you and waiting for any chance to get rid of you. I tried to stop him. Really, Belinda. I did."

Even though they happened months ago, memories of their past conversations registered like they'd happened a few hours before. The National Institutes of Health awarded Dr. Robert Winn a contract for seven million dollars based on her research. Not to mention the fat six-figure salary and stipend Winn would receive.

Heat flushed her cheeks, and her body trembled at his betrayal. She'd worked on the project for years. She wrote the contract proposal and when she lowered her guard, he swooped in and stole everything.

But the contract wasn't the biggest blow. It was his application for a patent. A patent that would not only secure billions of dollars from the oil industry, but probably put Winn in the running for a Nobel Prize. Belle didn't care about the money or the awards. Her passion was developing innovative technology to enhance lives using fewer chemicals. And oh, how she could help people with that type of financial backing.

"Why do you care about my new research? You already have the biofuel project."

"You will *not* show me up, Belinda!" He screeched the words. "You think you're smarter than me? You're not! I will not let you ruin me!"

Realization clicked into place. Robert was the protector, but Bobby was a narcissist. "It's okay, Bobby. Calm down." She lowered her voice to a soothing tone. "I'm not smarter than you. Look how easily you found me and brought me here."

"Don't tell me to calm down! You don't tell me what to

do!" Rage filled his voice. He ignored the gun she aimed at his chest and bored his eyes into hers.

Adrenaline thrummed through Belle's veins and surged into every muscle. She'd stepped on some kind of invisible land mine. One wrong move and Bobby would explode into Robert, the psychopath who wanted her dead.

It was time to leave. Staying this long was a mistake. It didn't matter what his motives were. Life was worth more than knowledge, and it was time to go. Now.

Belle shuffled her feet backward. "Bobby…I…I…" Her mind grappled for the right words to say.

Bobby tilted his head and narrowed his eyes.

Then Belle heard it too. The faint sounds of rustling foliage.

"Jonah," she whispered.

"In here," she shouted. "Jonah, I'm in here!"

A throaty snarl roared from Bobby as his expression twisted into a flinty stare. He lunged for the rifle in the middle of the room. Belle was quicker and slammed her foot on the barrel before he could reach it.

"Get back!" she yelled.

Bobby scrambled to his feet and roared again. He threw his weight at her knees and knocked her off-balance. Belle crashed to the floor, and he climbed on top of her, pinning her hands to the ground. She drove her left foot into the dirt and pivoted her hips. Rolling to her side, she flipped Bobby over onto his back and brought her knees into a fetal position. She smashed both feet into his ribs with all her strength and pushed away.

He released an involuntary scream as the wind forcefully left his lungs. Before she could get to her feet, he grabbed her calf and yanked her down.

His nails dug into her flesh, and she screamed as white-hot pain burned through her leg. A hot trickle of blood dribbled into her shoe. Bobby's death grip fueled her into a blind rage. She slammed the butt of the gun into his face. His nose burst into an explosion of blood as the bone and cartilage shattered. He released her leg and covered his face with both hands. He howled and writhed in pain.

Still holding the pistol, Belle stretched to the right and grabbed the rifle. Climbed to her feet and ducked beneath the strap and repositioned it onto her back. The motion made her head spin and she paused to let a wave of dizziness pass. Bobby rammed her from behind with a grunt. Grabbed her wrist and tried to wrench the gun free.

Belle managed to raise her gun hand over her head and drop her other arm while twisting to face him. She brought her gun hand down, trapping his wrist under her arm. Bobby threw his weight back, dragging her to the floor. She landed facefirst on his chest with a yelp.

His dark eyes blazed with fury. He'd switched. It wasn't Bobby she wrestled with. It was Robert, and he planned to kill her.

They wrestled on the floor, the gun trapped between them. She struggled to drag her gun hand free, but his hands coiled around her fingers squeezing tight.

The gun in her hand boomed in an explosion of light and heat in the dark cellar.

Jonah flinched when the gunshot pierced the air. He didn't have to follow Oscar now. The blast sounded from beneath his feet. He bolted down the slope, blindly running while navigating the boulders and bramblebushes. He slipped on a loose rock, fell and got up.

"Slow down," Riley called. "You'll be no help if you break a leg."

Ignoring his words, Jonah leaped from the top of the

hill to the ground below. He landed hard and rolled to absorb the impact. He bounded to his feet and saw that Oscar had beaten him to the cellar door. The dog barked and pawed at the threshold.

Riley skirted around Stella. "Call it in and wait in the field 'til backup arrives."

"Oscar, Wait!" Stella called from the top of the hill. The dog instantly stopped and put his rear to the ground.

Following his gun, Jonah inched the door open. It took a second for his eyes to adjust to the darkness, but he could make out two figures on the ground. There, in the middle of the room, Belle was slumped over another body with a rifle strapped to her back. A pool of blood seeped into the ground around her. The sight hit Jonah like a gut punch.

He couldn't see the suspect's face, but kept his gun aimed and stepped farther into the damp room.

"Belle? Belle, are you okay?"

He took another cautious step forward but froze when he sensed a shadow in his periphery. Over his shoulder, he saw Riley in the doorway.

Riley had his gun trained at the bodies on the ground. "I'm covering ya," he said.

Jonah clicked his gun into its holster and rushed to Belle. Delicately, he rolled her onto her back and saw the pistol fall from her hand. A dark red circle of blood stained the center of her shirt.

No...no...no...

He reached to check signs of life but stopped short when her eyelids fluttered open. Her big blue eyes blinked and focused on his face. Jonah's pulse sputtered. "Where were you shot?"

"I...I wasn't."

"Oh, thank You, God." He drew Belle into his arms

and cradled her head. She lifted her arm and stroked his cheek. He captured her hand and brought it to his lips, kissing her fingers. "I thought I lost you."

"I'm right here," she said.

Riley cautiously shuffled into the room and squatted beside them. He pressed two fingers against the man's neck. "He's alive. Get the gun while I secure him."

Jonah lowered Belle and took the offered glove from Riley. He didn't waste time putting it on. Instead, he used the glove to pick up the gun and drop it into the plastic evidence bag Riley held out to him.

For the first time, Jonah looked at the kidnapper, prepared to come face-to-face with his twin brother, Malachi Pry. Recognition didn't flare. In fact, this guy looked nothing like Malachi. "Wait, who is this?"

"It's my colleague, Dr. Robert Winn." Belle lifted herself off the ground and got to her feet. She winced and grabbed her stomach.

Jonah reached out and steadied her. "What's wrong? I thought you weren't shot."

"I think it's a bruise or something. We were on the ground with the gun between us when it went off."

"You better let Jonah have that rifle." Riley gestured to the weapon still hanging from her back. "Use that glove I gave you and leave it by the door. Abe can collect it as evidence."

Jonah helped Belle by lifting the gun strap over her head. He used the glove to carry the rifle, barrel down, to a spot near the door and far away from the suspect.

Behind him, Winn coughed. Small droplets of blood trickled from the corner of his mouth. The man didn't look good.

Riley was on the radio, asking for assistance. He lifted his chin at Jonah. "Get on outta here so I can secure the scene. Have Stella take a look at Belle and let her know I've got a LifeLine chopper incoming for a GSW. I'll ride with Winn and meet you at the hospital."

Jonah acknowledged Riley's orders and wrapped an arm around Belle's shoulders. "Think you can walk?"

She nodded, took one step and wobbled. "I guess I could use a little help."

He planted a soft kiss on the top of her head and guided her outside. The sunshine stung his eyes and beneath his arm Belle ducked her head. With a hand over his eyes to create a visor, he looked for Stella.

Stella waved an arm over her head. "Over here."

Oscar chewed his toy near her feet.

In Jonah's opinion, the dog deserved an entire steak dinner as a reward for finding Belle, but he'd make that offer to Stella later.

Talia sat half in and half out of her park ranger UTV with one leg bracing herself on the ground. She talked into the radio connected to the dash of the kitted-out medical transport vehicle.

Jonah had never seen anything like it. The rugged UTV had six knobby tires and an open-air cab. The back had two fixed tool kits on each side and a rear-facing seat beside an orange rescue basket for a paramedic to ride with the patient.

Deputy Lightfoot gave Jonah a nod as he rushed by with a medical kit.

The distinct thumping of helicopter rotors grew louder, and Jonah turned to see the red-and-white air ambulance in the sky. The chopper passed overhead, circled, then set down in the field. Paramedics hopped out the side door with a stretcher and rushed into the cellar.

Things were moving fast, and Jonah had a million questions for Belle, starting with how she'd managed to get the rifle away from Winn. And how he ended up with a gunshot wound in his stomach. There would be time for questions later. Right now, he needed to hand her over to Stella and let the rescue team do their jobs.

But where did that leave him?

Sabbatical.

Chase made it clear. Jonah had to separate himself from Belle and go back into hiding. The case he'd been working depended on it. If he wanted to return to his undercover role and bring down the drug cartel's operation from the inside, he had to step back. He wasn't here as an FBI agent.

Stella closed the distance and looked like she wanted to give Belle a hug but thought better of it. "Oh girl, I'm so glad you're safe!"

"Thank you for finding me… Again." She smiled and slipped out of Jonah's arms to give Stella a hug.

Oscar barked.

"I think Oscar is feeling left out," Jonah said.

Belle released Stella and gave Oscar an exhausted smile. "I'd give you the biggest hug, but I'm not sure I can manage it just now."

"Here," Stella said. "Come sit and let me take a look at you. You survived your ordeal, but I see your sutures didn't."

Jonah guided Belle to the UTV and helped her sit on the edge. Voices from behind drew his attention. The paramedics jogged to the chopper with Winn strapped to a stretcher. Riley followed, ducking beneath the rotating blades before he climbed inside. A medic slammed the doors shut and Jonah watched the helicopter disappear into the sky.

Stella blotted the cut on Belle's forehead, and she sucked air between her teeth. Seeing her in pain tore at his heart. And now he would be the one inflicting pain when he said goodbye.

He rubbed the back of his neck and looked at the ground, searching to find the words to tell Belle this was the end of the road for them. No way could he go into the city and risk someone recognizing him. His shaggy hair and beard only went so far to mask his identity.

Rubbing the toe of his shoe into the dirt, he told himself to say the words. Do it quick like ripping off a Band-Aid. "Belle... Belle, I—"

"Riley's on the radio," Talia said. "He's asking you to escort Belle to the hospital since he and Deputy Lightfoot will be tied up with the crime scene for a while. He says he's cleared it with Special Agent Bishop."

Jonah snapped his jaw shut and blinked at Talia. The park ranger leaned her head forward in anticipation of his answer.

"Of course, he's going with me," Belle said. "Jonah wouldn't leave me after everything that's happened. Right, Jonah?"

Without his permission, his head bobbed in agreement and he fought the urge to pump his fist in the air. Now he'd have to buy *two* steak dinners. One for Chase and one for Oscar.

He tried to smother the grin but gave up and smiled wide. "Tell the sheriff, nothing would make me happier than to escort Belle to the hospital."

SIXTEEN

Belle recoiled from the icy touch of the stethoscope on her chest. "Oh, that's cold!"

"Sorry," Dr. Chambers said. "I should've warned you. Deep breath in…hold it…and release."

The doctor repeated the procedure, listening to Belle's heart and lungs.

After hearing everything Belle went through over the past few days, the doctor had insisted she stay at least one night for observation. A plastic surgeon had taken care of repairing the cut on her temple and said the scar would be nearly imperceptible after it healed. Belle had been poked and prodded for the past twenty-four hours and she was ready to leave.

When Dr. Chambers finished, she pulled the stethoscope out of her ears and draped it around her neck. She scribbled a note in Belle's medical chart then closed it. "Well, all your tests look great. Brain scans, blood work, psychological and cardiovascular tests—everything is normal. If you're ready, I think we can get you out of here sometime tonight."

"That sounds great," said Belle. "And the amnesia?"

Doctor Chambers hugged the folder to her chest and studied Belle. "We can't be sure if the amnesia stemmed from your head injury and subsequent concussion, or if it was brought on by the extreme psychological trauma of your attack. There are a lot of unknowns with sudden amnesia, but the EMDR you did with Dr. McGee seems like it helped. Give it some time." She patted Belle's foot. "You need to rest, and let your body heal. The memories should continue to return in time."

"How would I know when all my memory returns? I don't even remember what I've forgotten."

Dr. Chambers smiled. "Well, you're not alone there. I feel the same way about a few of my college math classes."

They laughed and Belle twisted the blanket in her hand. Memories continued to return, but pieces of her life were missing. The FBI located her parents in Australia, but it took a photo and a phone call for Belle to remember they'd moved there to help her older sister and brother-in-law with their new baby.

The lost memories filled her with sorrow, but she was thankful for new ones. Memories that included Jonah. And Stella and the small town of Piney Village. How could she return to her old life as if nothing happened?

"Well, I'm not sure how the amnesia will affect my job. But as you know, I'm taking time off. A *lot* of time off." She tilted her head to the left, indicating the FBI agent guarding the door outside her room. "I guess there's time to work everything out."

"Things like where you keep the flour, where you shop and your favorite brand of toothpaste. Those things can be relearned. Therapy could help with the rest. Or…you go on living your life." She shrugged. "It's up to you."

"I guess I have a unique opportunity to discover who I'm truly meant to be instead of living with past regrets."

"I'd say that's the blessing in the midst of this." She grinned and checked her watch. "I have to finish my rounds.

A nurse will check on you and we'll get you discharged soon."

"Thanks, Doctor."

A few minutes later there was a light knock at her door. "Come in."

Belle's heart fluttered. It wasn't the nurse. It was Jonah.

"Sorry it took me so long, but I had to sweet talk Chase into bringing us dinner since I'm under strict orders to stay inside the hospital."

He placed a brown paper bag on the tray table and repositioned it over her lap.

"That smells delicious." She moved her feet to make room for Jonah and patted the bed. "Sit."

Jonah sat and pulled their burgers and two water bottles out of the fast-food bag and arranged the items on the table between them. "I didn't know what soda you like so I hope water is okay."

"Water is perfect, thank you." She bit into her cheeseburger and her taste buds exploded. Her shoulders fell and she closed her eyes savoring the bite. An audible sigh slipped out.

He chuckled. "It's good?"

"*So* good," she said around a mouthful.

They ate in silence. The air between them crackled with energy and Belle hesitated to say anything to ground them.

Jonah had stuck beside her during the transport down the mountain to the ambulance waiting on a nearby road and all the way to the hospital. When she woke this morning, he was stretched out asleep in the recliner beside her bed.

He crumpled his empty wrapper and tossed it in the bag. "How's the pain today?"

"It's good. Sore." The closeness of the gunshot left her

with a softball-sized bruise and a pretty good burn from the muzzle blast. At least the bullet fired away from her. Robert hadn't been so lucky. "Any update on Robert?"

"May I?" He gestured to her trash, and she nodded. After he cleared the tray table, he rolled it away and scooted closer, now sitting by her side.

"Last I heard, Winn made it through surgery and he's recovering. Chase will be back to interview him, but I doubt I can be present given Winn's intent to kill a federal agent."

She dropped her head. "I'm sorry I shot him, but I'm thankful we're safe."

"He kidnapped you and held you captive. You struggled and the gun went off. He would have killed you if you hadn't been so smart and calm." He took her hand and gave it a reassuring squeeze. "But listen, I wanted to say something—"

"Me too," she hurried to interrupt him. She had no idea where he would take the conversation, but she wanted to make sure he knew how much he meant to her. "Do you mind if I go first?"

"Not at all."

She swallowed. He was sitting close. Close enough to hear her pounding heart. It unsettled her. "Jonah, I know I'm responsible for destroying your quiet life, burning down your cabin and nearly getting you killed...*several* times. But I'm so glad it was you who found me that day."

"It's the best thing to ever happen to me." His smile stole her breath.

Oh, why didn't they meet on her hike the week before all this happened? She was right there at the same lake every single week for months and never once did they meet.

Well, she couldn't dwell on that when there was so

much ahead. "Agent Bishop and I spoke last night. I remembered why you looked so familiar to me. I'd seen your twin brother, Malachi, attacking that woman."

"Valerie Davidson."

"Yes, I remember everything about it. I don't know why but I rushed toward them, interrupted him before he killed her. Screamed for him to stop. I...I...took his picture."

She searched Jonah's eyes. The same familiar eyes she'd seen that fateful night. The eyes she captured in a photograph and turned over to the FBI.

But Jonah's eyes were different. Soft and warm. Malachi's eyes were cold and dead. The only thing the two men had in common was their appearance.

She swallowed. "Even though Robert kidnapped me, I'm sure it was Malachi who attacked me in the woods. I saw him. He's the one who pushed me off the bluff. I'm sorry for ever thinking it was you."

"It's understandable. We *are* twins." He shifted closer. "Chase says they've located Malachi and he'll be arrested soon."

"I caused you so much trouble."

He leaned closer and swept her hair away from her eyes with a soft stroke. "You're no trouble." His voice was a husky whisper. "I'd do anything within my power to help you."

Every muscle in her body buzzed at his touch. Her throat went dry, and she licked her tingling lips. She held his gaze and leaned in, their noses nearly touching. His hot breath swirled the space between them and caused her skin to prickle.

"If Malachi will be arrested soon," she breathed, "then we can—"

Jonah snapped his head back and blinked. He jumped

away from the bed and rocked back on his heels. Ran his hands through his hair. "Belle, we can't. This isn't a good idea. My job…and you're a witness in the case against my brother. If we—"

"I know, I know. You're right. It could ruin the whole case." She sat up straighter and pulled her legs under.

"It's more than that, Belle. I don't live a normal life. I've been working undercover on a case for a long time. When I'm undercover I'm a different person. I do things…" He ran a hand over his beard and blew out a breath.

"We don't have to decide right now. Once the trial is over—"

"I'll go back to work."

His words hit Belle like a slap in the face.

She blinked, then nodded. Understanding dawned. His job came first. It was more important than their relationship. More important than her. She was willing to wait until the trial was over, but by then Jonah wouldn't be there. Betrayal stabbed at her heart. How could she be so blind?

"Maybe you're right," she said. "We don't know each other at all. The *real* us. We've been living this life forced upon us by circumstances and let's face it, it's not who we are. You're an FBI agent and I'm a…a phycologist."

He took a step toward her. "I wanted more time with you. More time with the *real* you."

"Me too," she whispered.

She didn't know what else to say. Their time together was over. Once the hospital discharged her, the agent would drive her home and she'd probably never see Jonah again.

She bit her lip and blinked back the tears threatening to spill out.

Jonah shuffled to the edge of her bed and took her

hands again. They trembled slightly at the feel of his warmth. "I like you, Belle. I really, *really* do. I love who I am when I'm with you. Belle—"

"See, that's the problem," she said, pulling her hands away. She lifted her chin and drew herself up. "My name's not *Belle*."

Jonah pushed out of Belle's room and caught his toe on the chair in the hallway. He stumbled, but quickly regained his balance. Perfect. Belle had really thrown him off his game and that last remark? Oh, it made his blood boil. If anything, it solidified his decision to distance himself from her even though his heart didn't agree.

He stuck a hand in his hair, squeezed his eyes shut and emitted a low growl.

"Problem?" Zeke Harrison, the agent stationed in the chair outside Belle's room, glared at him but didn't bother to get up.

Older than Jonah by about ten years, Zeke had a gray goatee and short gray hair that only made his ever expanding forehead look bigger. No one would take him for a federal agent in his black polo shirt, dark jeans and well-worn cowboy boots.

Jonah knew Zeke from prior cases, and he'd always liked the guy.

"Just… Women," Jonah muttered, dropping his hand from his hair.

Zeke shook his head and waved both palms. "Say no more." He folded his arms across his chest and studied Jonah for a moment. "You know, there's a chapel on the second floor if you need a place to talk things out."

Jonah almost laughed at the suggestion. Zeke clearly didn't want to be Jonah's sounding board. He couldn't blame the guy. Things were complicated. "Thanks, I think I'll head there. I need to clear my head."

"Yeah." Zeke snorted. "Let me know how that works out for ya."

Jonah spun on his heels and marched to the end of the hall. He stabbed the elevator call button with his finger and waited. Hands on hips.

Belle didn't understand the life of an undercover FBI agent. Gone for weeks at a time with limited connection to anyone other than his team. When he joined the FBI, he never expected to work undercover, but he had a real opportunity to make a difference in the world. To bring down a violent drug cartel and save innocent lives.

The doors opened and Jonah stepped into the empty elevator and hit the button for the second floor. He leaned his head back on the wall and pictured Amy. For some reason his memory wouldn't let him remember her as the lively girl he met and fell in love with in college. No, when he closed his eyes, he pictured Amy's waxen face and vacant eyes staring into nothingness.

All because of him.

The elevator opened and Jonah followed the sign to the chapel. He slipped inside and dropped into the back pew. Jonah dropped his face to his hands and hunched over. Why did thoughts of Amy keep coming to mind? He'd put all that behind him almost two years ago.

The chapel door creaked, and Jonah turned to see Chase.

"About time you started praying again." He slid into the pew in front of Jonah and faced him, one elbow propped on the backrest.

"I wasn't praying," Jonah mumbled. "Why are you here?"

"More importantly, why are *you* in *here*?" He looked around the chapel.

Jonah leaned back. "I don't know…I can't stop thinking about Amy."

"I know you blame yourself, but her death isn't your fault."

"I should have been there. I was *supposed* to be there. But no. I let the job come first, just like when my mom died."

"The job is what it is, but you can't put your life on hold based on that. What are you thinking? You'll stay home all day waiting for something bad to happen to your loved ones? Meanwhile, other innocent people die because you chose to sit back and do nothing?" Chase became more animated, his words more urgent. "Where's your faith, man? This is nonsense and deep down you know better than this."

"Wait a minute." Jonah narrowed his eyes. "Less than twenty-four hours ago you said my entire career was on the line because of my feelings for Belle."

"Feelings for— Ohhhh! Is *that* what this is about?" Chase threw his head back and laughed.

"You think this is funny?"

"A little, yeah."

Jonah looked away and clamped his lips together to bite back a retort. Chase was his friend, but he was also his supervisor and deserved respect.

"Listen, man. I know your faith isn't as strong as it used to be," Chase continued.

"Yeah." Jonah snorted.

Chase ignored him. "My warning yesterday was meant to keep your head in the game, not keep you from falling in love and having a life. The case against Malachi is strong, but it's not *your* case, remember? That lumberjack thing you've got going on can only go so far to hide your identity. If someone sees you and calls the police claiming you're the Trailside Strangler, your entire life will go public. The cartel will know we're on the inside. Your undercover days will be over, and our case will go nowhere. I don't have to remind you what they're capable of. They *will* come after you."

If Chase knew how dangerous the cartel could be, then why didn't he understand why Jonah wouldn't get close to Belle? "I think you're making my point," he said.

"Let me give you a little advice, something my friend in the agency said when I was a rookie agent. You cannot do this job without God. Okay, so hear me out on this," he said.

"Think of yourself as a pilot. You know your aircraft inside and out. You're highly skilled and highly trained. You have a destination in mind and you're in control of the aircraft. But without the voice of God guiding you, sort of like an air traffic controller, you might not see the other planes in the air before it's too late. He'll navigate you through the storms and keep you on the right path. Without God, you'll veer off course and find yourself somewhere you never wanted to be."

"Or crash and burn," Jonah finished.

Chase slapped Jonah's knee. "Exactly."

It would take some time to process everything Chase said, but it made sense. Dad used to make a similar reference to God and using Him as the compass to follow. How'd he forget that? "I guess somewhere along the way I stopped trusting God and started trusting myself. But yeah, I don't have the whole picture and I think it's time to start listening to the one who does."

"That's good, man." Chase's features hardened and he laced his fingers. "But hey, I didn't come in here to preach at ya. I wanted to update you on my interview with Winn."

Jonah sat up straighter and leaned in.

"That guy is a piece of work." Chase rubbed his jaw. "We really struggled to get coherent facts from him, especially about the attacks. I think we'll have to interview him with a whole team of experts present, and even then, we might not get a full statement."

"Did he say why he tried to kill Belle?"

"I guess Winn thought she would turn him in for fraud. I couldn't tell if he was trying to stop her from turning him in because he'd lose the money, or simply because he couldn't stand the thought of being disrespected."

"Sounds like one personality tried to protect the other one. That's how they generally work in people with dissociative identity disorder, right?"

"Yep, but what doesn't make sense is he only confessed to some of the attacks. He wouldn't cop to all of them."

"Really?"

"He was adamant that he wasn't the one who attacked Belle in the woods on the day you found her."

Jonah nodded. "It was Malachi. Belle is convinced the attacker looked like…like me. It's why she tried to run from my cabin at first."

"I don't think we can be one hundred percent sure about anything Winn says, but he said he followed her to Eagle Lake with the hope she would lead him to her secret research project. He saw a man wearing camouflage attack her."

"Matches what I saw." An idea struck Jonah like a thunderbolt. He jumped to his feet. "As long as Malachi is out there, Belle is in danger. I want to go into witness protection with her," Jonah blurted. "I can keep her safe."

Chase stood and put a hand on Jonah's shoulder. "Whoa, Jonah. Slow down. The marshals can handle protecting Belle. It's their job."

"I know. But I'm…I'm…" He grasped for something to say that would change Chase's mind. If he could spend more time with Belle, he could explain his feelings. "I'm supposed to be off-grid, remember? What's more off-grid than WITSEC? If nothing else, I deserve protection from the cartel."

Chase sighed and shrugged with his hands. "You may be too late. Zeke is moving her to a secure location as we speak." He made a show of checking his watch. "They're probably gone already."

"Make the call, Chase. Tell the marshals I'm going."

Jonah didn't bother waiting for a response. He dashed out of the chapel and ran flat out through the halls, bypassing the too-slow elevator. He rounded the corner, jerked the door open and burst into the stairwell. Taking two steps at a time, he sprinted up each flight of stairs until he reached the sixth floor.

Sweat dampened his back, making his shirt cling to his body. His chest heaved with each breath as he retraced his steps past the elevator and headed toward Belle's room. More patients in this area meant slowing his pace to a brisk walk to avoid crashing into anyone.

Jonah's stomach lurched when he saw Zeke's empty chair. Belle's door was open, and the lights were off. Her unmade bed meant they hadn't had time to clean the room. He knew it was futile but checked the bathroom anyway.

Nothing.

He was too late. Belle was gone, but she might still be in the building. If he hurried, there was a chance he could fix the colossal mistake he'd made by letting her go.

SEVENTEEN

Agent Zeke Harrison rolled Belle's wheelchair through the hospital, following a nurse. Belle protested using the chair, but the nurse said it was hospital policy and if she wanted to leave, she had to ride. They navigated the maze of corridors and ended up near the emergency room. Zeke paused at a heavy-duty glass door to let the nurse swipe her key card. The door opened to a covered parking area with several ambulances rumbling near the wider sliding glass doors of the ambulance bay.

Belle had missed the sunset and was surprised to see the ink-blue night sky. Lost in her thoughts about Jonah and everything she still faced with the serial killer trial, the time slipped by without her notice.

She regretted the harsh words she spoke to Jonah. It was a terrible way to end things, and if she were honest, she deeply missed him already.

"That's my vehicle," Zeke said, pointing to a dark-colored SUV parked in the circle drive.

The nurse helped Belle out of the wheelchair. "I hope you feel better," she said.

"Thanks, you too." She cringed as soon as the words were out. She'd just told the nurse she hoped she felt better which went to show how preoccupied her mind really was.

Zeke opened the back door and gestured for Belle to climb in.

She used the side step to climb into the massive vehicle and settled into the soft leather seat.

"You in?" Zeke asked.

She nodded and Zeke's phone rang. He answered the call and closed the back door.

Belle heard a voice shout, "Wait!"

Through the tinted window, Belle saw Jonah bursting out of the ambulance bay doors, running toward the SUV. Zeke stepped in front of Jonah, a protective hand up to stop him. She heard them speaking in muted tones but couldn't make out their muffled words.

Zeke opened her door. "Dr. Lewis, I have Special Agent in Charge Chase Bishop on the phone. He says Jonah will be traveling with us if you don't mind."

"I...I don't mind," she stammered. What had changed Jonah's mind? Or was this part of his case?

Zeke patted Jonah on the shoulder. "You almost missed your chance."

Jonah locked his gaze on to her. His features softened. "Yeah, I know."

Heat flushed her neck. She scooted to the middle and Jonah climbed into the backseat with her. Zeke shut the door and stood outside, talking on his phone.

"Listen, Bel—Belinda. I couldn't wait to see you."

She flinched. How could she have been so rude earlier? "No, Jonah." She placed her hand on his chest. "Don't call me Belinda. Call me Belle."

"But you said—"

"I know what I said, but maybe I wasn't thinking straight. I did have a head injury, you know."

"According to your brain scans, you can't use that as an excuse," he teased.

"Can't a girl catch a break after everything I've been through?"

Jonah laughed and pulled her in for a hug, resting his chin on her head. She liked how she fit in his arms.

"I guess I'll let it slide this time," he said.

"I'm sorry for what I said to you, Jonah. Belinda was the old me. God gave me a second chance, and I'm ready for a new life."

One that included Jonah if he'd allow it.

He released her and looked into her eyes. "There is something I need to tell you."

Her stomach clenched. "Okay, what is it?"

"I lost someone special. Someone besides my parents. Her name was Amy and—"

Zeke opened the driver's door and slid behind the wheel, no longer on the phone. "We need to get moving."

"Yeah, okay," Jonah said. He lowered his voice, "We will talk more later. I'm going to the safe house with you, so we'll have plenty of time once we're settled."

Zeke pulled out of the hospital onto the main road. "We'll swing by your house, Dr. Lewis. You can have a few minutes to pack a bag, then I'll take you to a secure location for the preadmittance briefing with US Marshals Service personnel. We're waiting on some paperwork from the US Attorney, then they'll take over the protection services."

"Thank you, Zeke, but do you know where I live?"

"Yes, ma'am. The FBI tends to know these things," he chuckled.

"Everyone seems to know more about my life than I do these days."

It might be strange to see her house after her memory loss. It could unlock the missing pieces of her recall. Bursts of memories could ignite, like when she saw Robert. But what would it be like with Jonah in her house? If she didn't recognize anything, if those memories of her home and her belongings were lost, he'd see it for the first time right along with her.

"Do you think witness protection is necessary?" Belle asked.

Belle caught Zeke staring at Jonah in the rearview mirror.

"What? What am I missing?" she said.

Jonah gripped her hand. "Until Malachi is arrested, we have to go above and beyond to ensure your safety."

"I heard Winn talking to someone when he carried me into the cellar. I thought there were two people, then realized he was talking to himself. Or at least I thought he was. Is it possible—"

"No, I don't think they were working together," Jonah said. "Winn said he followed you to Eagle Lake and witnessed the attack. That's when he got the idea to kill you and make it look like Malachi did it."

Belle rested her head on Jonah's shoulder. What was happening to her life? She did a good deed and saved that woman, only to become a target.

Zeke pulled off the highway and onto a narrow road that snaked up the mountain. Recognition flared and she found herself mentally tracing the next few turns.

"I remember my house." She stared at the blue two-story home she'd bought when she'd decided to move out of the city. "We're only a short drive to Eagle Lake."

Jonah squeezed her shoulder. "Sounds like your memory is returning."

Zeke pulled his SUV to the curb and parked.

"Let's get you inside," Zeke said. "You have five minutes to gather what you need."

Jonah hopped out and helped her down. He took her hand, and they followed Zeke across the lawn to her darkened porch. Funny, she thought she'd installed automatic lights and scheduled them to turn on at dusk. Was that a memory, or an observation? She wasn't sure.

Both men rested their hands on their weapons. Zeke opened the front door with a key, and Belle didn't bother to ask him where he got it.

Her breath hitched when she stepped inside. "My house," she breathed. Memories of buying the house popped in her mind. She remembered moving in. Decorating. The layout. Everything.

She moved to the kitchen island and picked up a stack of photos. "I remember my house, but I don't remember these."

The first photo turned her blood to ice. It was a picture of herself with Jonah on Stella's porch. The photo fell from her trembling hands and drifted to the counter. Jonah scooped it up and examined it. The next photo captured Winn in a white sedan near Rebecca's house. Jonah on the porch in the background.

"He's watching us. He's *been* watching us," Jonah said.

"Stay in the kitchen while I check the house," Zeke said.

"Oh!" Belle cried. The stack of photos fell out of her hand, and she pointed at the kitchen window. "There's someone out there!"

A figure in camouflage ran through her backyard.

"Jonah, stay with Belle and call for backup," Zeke shouted. He ran to the door and bolted after the man. "FBI, freeze!"

Jonah had his phone out. He crossed the kitchen and shut the door.

"What's that noise?" Belle asked.

He paused. "It sounds like your phone is ringing."

"I don't have a phone. I lost my cell in the woods and I never installed a land line."

Belle stared at Jonah. His features hardened.

Then she heard it.

A woman's muffled screams coming from upstairs.

Jonah handed his phone to Belle. "I'm going to check it out. Stay here and call Chase, then call 911."

He took two steps, but Belle followed right behind him. "No, stay here, Belle—it might not be safe," he whispered.

"No way. You're not leaving me here alone. What if he comes in through the back door?" Her voice shook along with her entire body.

"Fine, but stay behind me, and be quiet."

With Belle close behind, he cleared the room and moved to the staircase. The phone stopped ringing and they paused. He sensed Belle's warm breath on the back of his neck.

He placed his foot on the first step and the phone began ringing again. Jonah glanced at Belle, and she shrugged.

With his gun ready, he moved up the carpeted steps keeping his back to the wall. They paused in the darkened landing and listened. The muted cries and ringing phone seemed to be coming from the left. He turned and nodded in that direction.

Belle pointed to her chest and mouthed, *My bedroom.*

They rounded the banister and moved to the opposite wall. The phone stopped ringing again and they paused to listen. The hoarse cries for help grew frantic.

Jonah aimed his weapon and used his other arm to guide Belle to stand behind him. Keeping her sandwiched between him and the wall, they moved forward as one.

They reached Belle's bedroom and Jonah saw the door hanging open a few inches.

He motioned for Belle to wait, and she nodded.

Jonah took a deep breath to steady himself then cleared the doorway. When his eyes focused on the center of the room, his stomach dropped. He forced himself not to move.

On Belle's king-size bed was the woman Belle saved from Malachi. Valerie Davidson was blindfolded and gagged in the middle of the bed. Her arms and legs secured to the black wrought iron headboard with zip ties. She whimpered beneath the cloth in her mouth.

Jonah turned to Belle and put his mouth next to her ear. "Wait while I clear the room. Do you have a primary bathroom?"

Belle nodded sharply.

"Stay in the doorway. No matter what you see, I want you to wait until I say it's clear."

"Okay," she whispered.

Belle stepped into the doorway and even in the darkness, he could tell she tensed. He moved through the bedroom, thoroughly checking the entire area including the bathroom and closets.

"It's clear," he said.

Belle rushed to the bed. "Valerie, it's okay. Help is here," Belle said in a hushed whisper.

She began to remove the blindfold. At her touch, Valerie recoiled and screamed under her gag. She thrashed her head and jerked her arms, prepared to fight off her attacker.

"Valerie, it's okay. Help is here," Belle said.

Watching Belle calm the woman reminded him of the day he found Belle and all she went through. She didn't trust him, and Valerie wouldn't trust them either.

"Valerie, the FBI is here," he said. "We have help on the way."

"I'm going to remove your blindfold," Belle said.

Valerie nodded.

Belle slipped her hands beneath the woman's head and untied the knot. Jonah noticed the red marks around her throat and her eyes appeared sunken into their sockets. A reddish-purple color surrounded both eyes and Jonah couldn't tell she'd been hit or if she'd been crying. Probably both.

"I'm going to remove the gag now, Valerie. Please don't scream. The man who kidnapped you might hear."

Valerie began crying as Belle gently removed the gag from her mouth. Every touch from Belle's delicate hands caused Valerie to flinch.

Belle shifted her eyes to his. Tilted her head to the restraint. Working his way around the bed, he cut her zip ties with his knife, keeping his face angled away from Valerie. He figured it was best if she didn't see him. He could only imagine how traumatic it would be to see the twin brother of her kidnapper while she was still in shock.

Belle helped the young woman sit up. Valerie threw her arms around Belle's neck. She buried her face in Belle's hair and sobbed. The agent in him itched to preserve the crime scene, but he couldn't break the moment. Instead, he held his gun against his thigh and watched Belle comfort the crying woman.

"Shhhh, it's okay, Valerie. You're okay," Belle soothed. She rocked gently and glanced at Jonah. "We're safe now."

Were they safe? Zeke should've returned by now, and where was the backup? He reached in his pocket for his phone, then remembered he gave it to Belle. Distracted by the phone ringing, he'd never hit Send on his call.

"We need to call for an ambulance," he said. "You still have my phone?"

Still holding Valerie with one arm, Belle reached into her pocket and handed Jonah his phone.

He reached for it as another phone rang. Both women startled at the high-pitched sound.

Out of the corner of his eye, Jonah caught the light from a phone screen on the nightstand.

Valerie wailed louder.

Jonah dialed 911 on his own phone and hit Send. He handed it to Belle. "Here, request an ambulance and emergency police assistance."

He found a tissue and answered the ringing cell phone. The screen read Unknown Caller, but Jonah was sure he knew who was on the other end of the call.

He answered. "Hello?"

"Hello…*brother.*"

EIGHTEEN

Belle watched as the blood rushed to Jonah's face and the veins in his neck corded. His hand squeezed the phone at his ear. She couldn't hear his call, but deep down she knew it was Malachi. He was calling to taunt them.

"911, what's your emergency?"

Belle hadn't realized the call connected. "Yes, yes. We need an ambulance and...and police."

"What's your name, ma'am?"

Belle heard the clacking of keys in the background. Every nerve in her body seemed to be bursting with energy making it difficult to think. "It's...it's Belle," she said. "We need you to send the ambulance."

"Stay on the line, Belle. Is the victim breathing?"

"Yes, yes, she's breathing. Someone broke into my house and tried to kill her. I think he's here somewhere."

"Okay, Belle, can you confirm the address where you're calling from?"

"Address, oh...yes! I know it!" She surprised herself by rattling off her address from memory. She wasn't sure if she should tell the dispatcher that an FBI agent was on scene. They might not come if they thought Zeke and Jonah could handle it.

"Ma'am?"

"Yes, I'm here."

"Ma'am, we have two fire units on their way. I've requested police and emergency medical units—please stay on the line."

Fire? Why was she sending fire units? Did Zeke call?—the smell of burning wood and ash registered and she twisted to look at Jonah. Clenching the phone to his ear, he scowled and stormed across the room to the window overlooking her backyard.

"Jonah, I think the house is on fire!"

The window exploded and Belle screamed. A bottle with a tail of fire smashed against the headboard and shattered. Liquid sprayed the curtains and the mattress. The fabric burst into flames.

"Get back!" Jonah shouted.

Belle jumped off the bed. Her eyes bulged at the rapidly spreading fire. The phone slipped from her fingers and fell to the floor.

"Oh, no!" Belle cried. "Get Valerie!"

Jonah scooped Valerie off the bed with both arms and turned toward the door. The sobbing woman buried her head into his shoulder.

"Let's go! We gotta get out of here!"

The window behind Belle ruptured and she screamed. She covered her head and turned to look. A bottle with a burning fuse sticking out of the top rolled on the carpet. She ran to Jonah and before they reached the door, a concussive blast rocked the house.

The floor beneath her feet shuddered and her arms flew out to balance herself. "What was that!"

"I don't know. Some sort of homemade explosive device? It doesn't matter. Go! I've got Valerie."

Belle was first into the hall. Black smoke rolled in the staircase and she tasted ash. "Jonah, there's smoke coming up the stairs."

"It's our only option," he said.

Sobs wracked Valerie's body and Belle nodded. "Go first—get Valerie out of here."

Jonah hesitated a beat.

"I'm right behind you," she said.

He turned and descended the steps with Valerie cradled in his arms. Halfway down the stairs, the smoke thickened and stung her eyes. She couldn't see anything. Not even the shape of Jonah. She fumbled for the handrail until she found it and used it to guide herself down the next step.

A loud crack rang out. The staircase buckled and shifted beneath her feet. She clutched the handrail. Squinted but couldn't see through the orange-black haze. The searing heat and thick smoke seemed impassible.

"Jonah…Jonah, where are you? I can't see you!"

The treads below her feet vibrated. Back upstairs or down? On instinct, she turned and darted up. The house shook and groaned. Two steps from the top, the staircase collapsed. She lunged for the landing and hit the floor on her stomach with a grunt.

Her legs dangled over open air. Skin-blistering flames raced to devour the fresh oxygen on the second level. Kicking her feet and squirming on her belly, Belle managed to pull herself onto the landing. Raced for her bedroom where she hid a fire ladder under her bed.

Flames engulfed her room and licked up the walls. No way could she get to the ladder. She winced at the intense heat and ducked. A bite of pain pricked her leg and she glanced down to see fire dancing on her pants and quickly patted the flames with her palms. Her palms burned, but she managed to extinguish it.

Coughing and inhaling hot smoke that burned her lungs and throat, she raced to the other side of the house and darted into her office. She slammed the door in a futile attempt to shut out the spreading fire. In the room she hesitated. All her sunscreen research and field notes were hidden here.

Maybe not.

An empty spot on her desk where her laptop should be. Piles of papers scattered. Bookcases toppled. Hardback journals filled with handwritten field notes scattered on the floor.

Smoke crawled through the edges of the door, slipping under the threshold and around the door casing. The fire was coming, and a lifetime of her field notes would be another victim.

Faintly, she heard Jonah screaming her name. Relief washed over her. He was alive, but still in the house.

"I'm okay!" she yelled. "Get out of the house—I'll meet you outside!"

Fighting the panic threatening to cripple her, she had to choose. Potentially face down a killer outside or stay here and burn to death. After a silent prayer asking God to prepare the way for her, Belle refocused and decided on a plan.

The bedroom had two windows. One led to the side of the house directly over the fence connecting her house to her neighbor's. If she jumped from there, she'd hit the fence.

She dashed to the window facing the backyard. Grabbed and yanked the curtains. They tore from the wall, bringing the rod on her head. She grabbed the metal pole and jabbed it into the window. Glass shattered. She swirled the rod around to clear the glass.

Fresh air rushed into the room. She sucked in a clean breath. The heat at her back intensified. The flames ate their way through the door. Hungry for oxygen.

She was running out of time.

With one arm, she scooped the curtains and draped them over the broken window. The heavy fabric dangled outside. The rod horizontally braced against the window, and she prayed it would hold. She climbed out feetfirst. Clutched the thick drapes and cautiously rappelled down the side of the house.

The fabric around two of the grommets tore and she slipped a few inches. Her breath hitched. She couldn't stop. Had to get to the ground. Hand over hand, she descended. A third grommet gave way. The curtain rod folded. Her anchor pulled free from the window frame, and she fell. Her legs drove through the shrubs planted alongside the house. Their sharp branches scraped and stabbed her body.

She hit the ground. The hard landing knocked the wind out of her. Wheezing and coughing, she tried to suck air into her lungs, but the muscles in her diaphragm refused to work. Around her, the yard was ablaze with red-and-orange-flickering light from the burning house, and she heard sirens blaring as if they were on top of her.

Her body began to cooperate, and she rolled over onto her side and drew in several deep breaths. Her eyes focused and saw the shape of a man.

Zeke's large frame curled on the ground beside her. Shirt wet with blood.

Belle scrambled on all fours. Placed two fingers under his jaw over his carotid. Over her own drumming pulse Zeke's throbbed slow and even.

"Zeke, can you hear me?" She snatched the curtains. Wadded them up and pressed at the wound on his side. "You're okay, Zeke. Just stay with me. Help is on the way."

A shadow approached from behind. Two strong hands shot out and jerked her to her feet.

Jonah coughed and rolled over. Pulled himself onto his hands and knees. He hacked from deep in his throat and spit a lump of ashy phlegm onto the floor. The last thing he remembered was calling to Belle after climbing out of the rubble from the collapsed staircase. He spun around and saw Valerie sprawled near the front door. A red-hot board on her legs. Flames encircled the carpet around her.

He ran to Valerie and heaved the board off, burning his hands. The intense temperature in the room boiled the sweat droplets on his skin. Dust and debris rained from the ceiling. Fiery coals landed and scorched through his shirt. The flesh on his back blistered. He ignored the pain and snatched a smoldering blanket off the floor. Covered Valerie's legs and smothered the flames at her feet.

The front door exploded inward with a crash. Two firemen rushed through the opening.

"Sir, sir! We're here to help," one of them called. "Let's get you two out of here."

Jonah tried to speak. His throat burned and all he could manage was a raspy cough.

One of the firemen lifted Valerie and cradled her in his arms. They disappeared through the thick smoke.

With the help of the second fireman, Jonah made it outside in time to see a black SUV slide to a stop in the street. Chase sprang from the car and ran to Jonah.

Over the blaring sirens the fireman yelled, "Is there anyone else in the house?"

"Where are Belle and Zeke?" Chase asked.

"I don't…I don't know…Zeke was outside and Belle

was right—" The phone in his pocket rang. With a shaky hand, he fished it out.

His nostrils flared and he punched the screen to accept the call on Speaker.

"Come out back, *brother*," the caller sneered.

Jonah spun on his heels.

"Stop, Jonah!" Chase called. "Wait for backup."

"You're the backup!" Jonah drew his weapon as he bolted to the side of the house.

Red-orange flames crawled over Belle's once beautiful home. The heat almost as severe as inside the house. He covered his eyes with his forearm and sprinted to the fence. Tried to hop over but caught his foot and fell on his shoulder. Scrambled to his feet and ran flat out to the backyard.

There, in the middle of the yard, he came face-to-face with his twin brother.

Jonah's muscles went rigid.

Malachi held Belle against his chest. Arms pinned to her sides. Her feet hovered off the ground. She thrashed and kicked but Malachi held tight. Jonah's heart ached at the fear in Belle's features.

"If you don't stop squirming, I'll snap your neck," Malachi growled into her ear.

Jonah studied his brother down the barrel of his gun. It was strange to see someone who looked like himself standing only a few feet away. Malachi wore camouflage pants and an army-green shirt. The light from the burning house cast an eerie glow over his dark eyes.

Chase appeared in Jonah's peripheral vision, weapon drawn.

"Well, well, well. We finally meet, brother."

"Let her go, Malachi!"

"Oh, you finally know my name after all this time pretending you didn't remember me."

"I didn't remember you. I didn't even know—"

A memory appeared to Jonah. A boy in the sandbox with him, playing with plastic horses and a metal tractor.

"Your face says you do remember me, brother. Stop pretending, *Jonah*!" He snarled Jonah's name.

"Why are you doing this? Why Belle?"

Malachi moved his mouth close to Belle's cheekbone and she whimpered "This pretty little thing? Belinda? She stuck her camera in my business and now she has to pay."

Jonah took a step toward him. "You could have let everyone believe it was me in that photograph."

"I'm not stupid, brother! You think the police are smarter than me? They don't even know what I'm capable of. I found you a few years ago and I watched you. I knew you worked for the FBI. Boy, I thought you were smarter than that, but apparently, I got all the brains, and you got the looks." He shook his head and laughed.

The sound grated on Jonah's nerves.

Two local law enforcement officers took up positions along the fence.

A mist of water bounced off the house and rained down. The firemen were extinguishing the fire. Cold drops of water landed on his bare skin, stinging the seared flesh on his back. The pain was excruciating, but if he could keep Malachi talking a little longer…

"Why did you kill all those women, Malachi?"

"What can I say? It amuses me."

Jonah shivered at his callousness. How could they be related? He moved a step closer. "Listen—"

Malachi took two steps away. "No, YOU listen! You're going to drop that gun and tell all your police buddies to put down their weapons or I break your little girlfriend's neck." He readjusted his big hands with one on

Belle's forehead and one on her chin, still holding her off the ground.

"No! Don't do it, Malachi." Jonah held both hands out, letting his pistol lie flat against his right palm. "The moment you kill her, these cops will pump your body full of bullets."

"So, I'll leave and take her with me." He took slow steps in retreat, darting his gaze from Jonah to the officers surrounding him.

"No, Jonah! Don't let him take me," Belle cried.

"That's not how this ends and you know it," Jonah yelled. "I can't let you take her. There's only one way out of this. Give yourself up."

"The way I see it, there are several ways this ends. You'll just have to decide if you'd rather watch me kill Belinda, or if you'd rather find her like you found Amy." He repositioned his arm and held Belle with his forearm around her throat.

Jonah's vision clouded red, and his heart cantered inside his chest. He brought his gun up and aimed at Malachi's head. His finger itched inside the trigger guard. He couldn't take a shot. No one could. It was too risky while he shielded himself with Belle.

"What do you know about Amy?" Jonah growled through clenched teeth.

"Ahhhh…Amy." Malachi's voice went nostalgic with some sick memory. "She was one of my firsts. Still trying to find my…*style* you know?" He grinned flashing his white teeth.

"You…you killed…" Jonah couldn't finish. His stomach hit the floor and he thought he might be sick. He swallowed and took two steps forward.

"She wasn't good enough for you anyway, brother. But

this one." He shook Belle. "Now she's a keeper. Smart *and* beautiful."

Malachi wanted to rile him up and toy with his emotions. But Jonah couldn't let him get under his skin.

Jonah sighed. "I just want to know my brother. I only found out I *had* a brother a few days ago. If only we could... If we could talk."

"And how do you reckon we do that? These guys aren't going to stand around and watch while we *bond*," he said.

"I'm a federal agent. I can get you into a mental facility. I can come visit you, get to know you there."

"Ha," Malachi laughed. "You'd really do that for me?"

"Of course, I would. You're my brother. We're blood."

Malachi stared at Jonah. Head slightly cocked. "Okay, brother." He released his hold and Belle dropped to the ground. He stuck his hands in the air and took two steps back.

"Hold your fire," Jonah yelled.

Chase echoed the command.

Belle scrambled to Jonah on her hands and knees.

Jonah stepped in front of Belle and studied Malachi. A wide grin slowly stretched across the face of his twin brother. Malachi slowly reached behind him.

Angry voices yelled, "Freeze! Don't move! Show me your hands!"

Malachi ignored them and brought his hand around in one fast, smooth motion.

Jonah fired.

The thunderous blast of gunfire splintered the night. Malachi's body crumpled to the ground.

NINETEEN

Belle squeezed her eyes shut. A split second before Malachi's body collapsed to the ground, she thought she saw a look of amusement on his face. It was one memory she didn't want to keep.

Shouts from the first responders registered as distant sounds. Jonah dropped to his knees beside her and pulled her close. Resting his chin on her head, he rocked her. A knot of sickness twisted her stomach. Her raw throat burned, and she couldn't tell if it was from the smoke inhalation or the sob trying to escape. Tears stung her eyes, but she held them in and nestled deeper into Jonah's embrace.

The fire-quenching water shot over the house, and she opened her eyes to see the spray arching over the burning roof and falling in the yard. The fire sizzled and cracked, breathing an ashy gray smoke into the sky. It plumed and drifted into the night as the water saturated the ground around them.

By now her home was a total loss. Whatever the fire didn't consume, the water destroyed. All her belongings, her journals, her years of laborious work… Gone.

Heaviness weighed in her chest at the loss. But it didn't matter. The only thing that mattered was being safe with

Jonah. They'd survived their ordeal and they'd done it together.

Radios squawked and she glanced around Jonah to see a uniformed officer helping a paramedic carry Zeke on a backboard. She tipped her head to look at Jonah, and realized his eyes were fixed on Malachi. On his stomach, hands cuffed behind him.

"I thought you killed him," she said.

Jonah shook his head slowly. "I couldn't do it. I shot him in the thigh."

A forensic photographer crouched nearby, capturing evidence in digital images before the water could wash it away. The camera flash popped. A glint of light illuminated an object near Malachi's head. A small metallic rectangle. Not a gun. Not a knife. A cell phone.

Belle couldn't wrap her mind around it. Malachi wanted Jonah to kill him, but Jonah spared his life. Her heart swelled. Jonah was an honorable man.

She couldn't stand to look at Malachi any longer and buried her head in Jonah's chest again. The smell of smoke and singed hair wafted from his skin. She gripped his arm and nuzzled underneath.

He shifted and sucked air between his teeth. It sent him into a coughing fit.

She studied him. Black soot smudged his arm muscles and his neck. Beneath the dirt and ash, he looked sunburned. Angry red blotches of burned skin dotted the areas where embers burned through his shirt.

"Jonah, you're burned. Your clothes…" She shook her head, unable to finish her sentence.

Jonah hesitated, then a smile spread across his face. "That's what you're focusing on? My clothes?" His voice was hoarse, and his brisk laugh turned into a cough.

He lowered himself to the ground, dragging her with

him. Laughter filled the space between coughs. The sound made her giggle and her pulse quicken.

The water continued to fall like rain and pooled around his head. She was over him, staring into his dark eyes. Droplets dripped from her nose onto his soot-covered face. Drenched, her wet hair hung limply and fell forward around them creating a curtain shielding them from the outside world. An intimate bubble where only they existed.

"Oh, ow," he said through a laugh. "It hurts when I laugh."

"I'm sorry, you must be in so much pain." She started to roll off, but he tightened his grip.

"No, please stay with me," he said.

Their laughing died and Jonah's features turned serious. His gaze held hers. "You bring so much joy to my life. Did you know that?"

"Really? So, being hunted, stalked, shot at and set on fire brings you joy?"

"Well, I *am* an FBI agent," he chortled.

She tapped his shoulder playfully. "Jonah!"

"I guess what I'm saying is I now see the difference between happiness and joy. I wasn't happy about the situations, but I still had joy in my heart, and I thank God you were by my side through it all."

"I know what you mean. And it makes my heart happy to know you're back on speaking terms with God."

Jonah smiled and pushed a strand of hair away from her face, only to have it fall again. "Belle, you and I aren't perfect, but you're perfect for me. I love you."

Her heart skipped a beat at his words. She tried to think of a witty response but all she could think about was the invisible magnet drawing her heart closer to Jonah. "I love you, too."

It was the worst possible moment, but she wanted nothing more than to kiss him. Their lips a mere whisper apart. His hot breath mingling with hers as they took slow rhythmic breaths together. It would be nothing to move a fraction closer and let her lips meet his in a warm kiss...

Footsteps came to a splashing halt beside Jonah's head and interrupted his special moment with Belle. Was she about to kiss him?

"C'mon, you two. Let's get you outta here," Chase said.

Reluctantly, Jonah eased his hold on Belle and Chase helped her to her feet. Her wet clothes clung to her and a blackened hole in her pants exposed her shin. The dampness made her red curls hang in long waves around her shoulders. Even with the blackened ash caked to her skin, Belle still looked beautiful to him.

Chase stretched his long arm toward Jonah. "Here, let me help you up."

Jonah grabbed Chase and pulled himself to his feet. Pain shot through his back as if the skin were being ripped from his bones. He couldn't suppress a cry.

"Jonah, are you all right?" Belle sucked in a breath. "Oh, your back..."

"It's...fine." He spurted a cough between each word.

"It's not fine—you need an ambulance," she said.

Chase frowned. "Yeah, man, you don't look so good."

"Yeah, okay." Jonah took one step and the ground dropped out from under him.

Chase caught him by the elbow and lowered him to the lawn. Jonah tried to ignore the pain screaming from every nerve ending, but it was overwhelming. Every inch of his back stung like millions of ravenous fire ants swarming his body. The torment threatened to steal his sanity.

"Medic! We need a medic!" Chase yelled.

In a flurry of activity Jonah couldn't keep track of, people swarmed around him. A cold metal stethoscope shocked his chest and a medic crouched beside him.

"My name is Dylan. Is it okay if I treat you?"

Jonah nodded and closed his eyes to stop his head from spinning. It made it worse, so he opened his eyes and focused on Belle. She stood behind the medic, hugging herself with a frown on her face.

"Can you tell me your name?" Dylan asked.

Jonah tried to speak but his throat burned, and he started coughing.

"His name is Jonah," Belle said.

"Okay, Jonah, don't talk right now. We'll take care of you from here."

Dylan cupped an oxygen mask over Jonah's nose and mouth. He breathed the clean air and felt his body tingle. Jonah's eyes fluttered and sleep tried to drag him down.

"Get him into the ambulance right away," Chase said. "This man is a federal agent, and I'd like him off the scene."

It was easier to breathe, but the world spun around him. Other voices called numbers and spoke too fast for his brain to comprehend. With assistance from the medics, Jonah moved to a stretcher and stared at the blackened sky. His skin was on fire, every nerve ending lighting up with pain.

"Jonah, it's okay. You'll be fine," Belle said in a worried voice. She gripped his hand.

He lolled his head to the side and saw the misery on her face. He wanted to comfort her, but his mouth wouldn't form words.

A male voice at his feet asked if he needed air transport.

"Negative. He's stable," Dylan said. "Jonah, I'm giving you something for the pain."

The pinch in his arm barely registered. Ice-cold liquid spread beneath his skin. The stretcher began to move, and Belle's fingers slipped away from his grasp. He called to her from beneath the oxygen mask, his words a muffled mess.

Overhead, flashing red-and-blue lights illuminated the faces jostling in and out of his line of sight. They paused and he heard the clatter of metal wheels being released followed by the sensation of his bed rolling. They must be on the driveway.

"We're loading you into the bus—you might feel a bump. Sorry about that."

The bed bounced and slid into the ambulance. Jonah closed his eyes and focused on breathing. The grogginess faded and he was aware of the pain in his back and chest, but it was tolerable.

"Okay, Jonah, ready for a ride to the hospital?"

"Not...without...Belle..." he breathed.

"I'm right here with you," Belle said. "I won't leave you."

The ambulance lurched softly, and Jonah sensed they were moving.

He opened his mouth and pushed air out instead of words. His throat hurt, but he tried again. "Care...bear..."

"What did you say?"

Beneath the mask he licked his lips and tried again. "By to care with," he stammered.

"Jonah, you're not making sense. Don't try to talk right now." Belle frowned. "What's wrong with him?"

"He might be confused. It's a side effect of smoke inhalation," Dylan said. "Give him a few more minutes on the oxygen. His head will clear. Best if he doesn't talk yet anyway."

Belle leaned over and whispered into his ear. "Don't talk now. Just listen."

She murmured words he couldn't quite understand. The sensation of her hot breath on his ear raised goose bumps on his arms. He tried to focus on her words coming faster now, spoken in a soft soothing tone.

Was she praying? Yes. He heard her as she prayed for healing of his wounds.

"God, please heal not only the burns on his body, but the scars on his heart," she whispered.

She ran her hand through his hair, combing it with her fingers. He closed his eyes and absorbed her words.

Finally, he gave in and silently prayed with Belle until he drifted to sleep.

TWENTY

Belle paced the corner of the emergency room waiting area and prayed for Jonah in hushed tones. She hadn't stopped praying for more than a few seconds since she'd climbed into the ambulance. Seeing his burned skin and the amount of agony he was in made her regret ever stepping foot into her house.

At least she could empathize with Jonah's waiting room experiences. After doctors treated her mild burns and injuries, they'd sent her back to the waiting room. An hour had passed without word on Jonah's condition. This was torture.

"Dr. Lewis? Is there a Dr. Lewis here?"

It took Belle a beat to realize *she* was Dr. Lewis. The name still seemed foreign, especially after being called Belle for the last few days. She turned to see a nurse in scrubs and clear-framed glasses, her dark hair piled high in a messy bun, surveying the room.

Belle waved. "I'm Dr. Lewis."

"Please follow me." She didn't wait for Belle but turned and scanned a key card on the reader. It beeped and the door opened automatically.

Belle traced the nurse's steps through a maze of hallways with endless doors and several nurses' stations.

The woman stopped at a doorway and gestured for Belle to go inside.

"Wait here—the doctor will be with you in a few minutes."

Belle thanked the nurse and watched her disappear down the hall.

Great. Another waiting room. Belle hugged herself and paced. She was restless and too wired to sit. The glass wall was designed to give an illusion of space, but it was still cramped. Suffocating. Her heart rate picked up speed and her pulse thumped hard in her head.

"I'm sorry to keep you waiting," Dr. Chambers said, startling Belle. "Please come with me and I'll take you to Agent Phillips."

Belle nodded dumbly. "I'm surprised to see you, Dr. Chambers. I wouldn't guess we'd have the same doctor."

"Well, I didn't mention it before, but I'm specially requested by the FBI to handle cases requiring discretion." She eyed Belle with a knowing look. "You must be going out of your mind with concern for your friend."

"I really am," she breathed. "How's he doing?"

They turned the corner and walked shoulder to shoulder down the beige hallway toward an elevator.

"Jonah's burns look worse than they are. We've cleaned and dressed his wounds, but as with most burn victims, infection is our biggest concern.

"There's good news and bad news, though. The bad news is his nerve endings weren't burned, so he'll feel the pain. But the good news is, he'll heal much faster and won't require surgery. We're keeping him a few days to monitor his pain and the infection."

"What about the smoke inhalation?"

"His lung X-rays look great, his throat is a little raw, but all in all he's in surprisingly good health."

Belle smiled. "Will he be able to talk?"

"He's alert and talking to the other agents now. They requested I bring you in to see him."

"I know confidentiality is an issue, but the woman who was in the fire with us, Valerie Davidson? Is she going to be okay?"

"I can't really say without breaking privacy laws, but the rumor is she's alive because of the two of you."

Belle understood. Valerie may be injured, but she would survive and that's all that mattered right now. Her physical wounds would heal, but her emotional wounds would last a lifetime. Something Belle knew all too well.

Dr. Chambers stopped at Jonah's room and Belle couldn't help but hug the pretty doctor. "Thank you for taking such good care of Jonah."

She smiled. "You're welcome. He must be really important to you."

Belle glanced over her shoulder to see Jonah sitting up in bed. "He is, Doctor. He really is."

Jonah's face lit when he saw her and he motioned for her to come in. Below the nasal cannula, patches of his mustache and beard looked singed. A white bandage covered most of his forearm and his entire upper body was wrapped in gauze. The sight of him stole her breath away. Tears pricked her eyes and she forced herself not to fall apart in front of him.

"You look like a mummy with all that gauze," she teased.

"Yeah, it's my new undercover look." Jonah chuckled, but it turned into a short cough that he covered with his fist.

Chase stood with his arms behind his back beside Sheriff Riley. Belle smiled at him. "Hey, Sheriff, I'm surprised to see you here."

Riley hugged her. "I'm only glad you're safe. Stella sends her love. She's in surgery with a Saint Bernard who needed help delivering her puppies."

"Puppies? I love puppies!" Belle cried.

Riley chuckled. "I told her about your house fire, and she wants you and Jonah to come stay with her for as long as you need."

Belle's heart melted and she hugged Riley again. "That is so generous. Tell her thank you."

There was more Belle wanted to say, but she didn't want to start crying.

"Here," Chase said, holding a cell phone. "This is your new phone. I've created contacts with emails and phone numbers for myself, Sheriff Riley and your friend Stella as well as a few others. I've also added a number for Jonah's temporary phone. I'm heading out for a while, tons of paperwork waiting for me. We have your initial statements, but I'll be in touch about a formal interview."

"Thank you so much," Belle said.

Chase paused and gave Belle a half smile. "I'm sorry for everything you've been through, but I'm glad you're safe."

"Me too," she said.

And she *was* sorry. Sorry for the whole series of events and for those who were hurt in the process.

"Before you go, any update on Valerie?" Jonah asked.

"She's in ICU but stable. Her injuries are severe, and the psychological stress took a toll. The doctors are keeping a close eye on her."

"Yeah, I know a little something about psychological stress," Belle said. "Can I go see her?"

Chase pinched his lips. "Her family is with her. I'd give it some time, let her come to you when she's ready."

"What about you, Belle, have all your memories returned?" Riley asked.

"I'm not sure I'll ever be able to answer that question." She shifted her weight. "I mean, how do you remember something you've forgotten?"

Jonah, Chase and Riley chuckled. She didn't mean it as a joke, but she smiled anyway.

"I'm off to brief the rest of the team on this resolution to our serial killer case," Chase said, heading for the door. "I'll be in touch."

"I'm heading out too," Riley said. "I've got my own mess to clean up with Dr. Winn."

When she was finally alone with Jonah, Belle sat on his bed and studied his eyes. Dark, but bright and alert. "How are you—"

"Belle, I have to tell you something."

Her breath caught. He had a habit of saying that, and in her experience those words were right up there with *we need to talk*. She wasn't sure she was ready for whatever he was about to say but nodded anyway.

"Malachi said something last night that I want to explain," he said.

"Oh, we don't need to talk about it right now."

"I'd like to…if you don't mind."

She nodded. "Okay, I'm listening."

He breathed in and exhaled a short cough. "I tried to tell you about Amy when we left the hospital." He paused and ran his tongue over his cracked lips. "Well, Malachi brought her up, but I…I didn't know…"

Belle didn't speak. She gave Jonah time to collect himself without interrupting him with the ten thousand questions firing off inside her head.

"Let me restart. I met Amy my first year of law school. She was an undergrad, but we dated a few years. When I graduated, I applied and made it into special agent training at Quantico. While I was there, I realized I wanted to marry her and told myself I'd propose after I completed training. But then my mom died and…it didn't seem like the right timing.

"After I became a special agent, I quickly found myself wrapped up in my first case. I planned to take a few days off to attend Amy's college graduation. I wanted to propose that weekend. I got hung up at work and I was a day late. I found her in her apartment. Someone murdered her. The police never even had a suspect."

A tear slipped along Belle's cheek. So much loss for one person to handle. She wanted to hug him, but worried about hurting his burns and took his hand instead.

"Malachi?"

He nodded. "Chase just confirmed. A unit went through his van and found…well, never mind. The point is, I blamed myself for not being there to save her."

"I don't even know how you can process something like that, Jonah." She shook her head. "No wonder you buried yourself in your job. It's a good escape."

"Yeah well, I think I'm done running," he said.

Belle tilted her head and searched his face for meaning. "What do you mean?"

"I just had a lengthy conversation with Chase about my job." Jonah blew out a slow breath. "After tonight, I'm done."

"Done? You can't be done with the FBI." Belle held his hand.

Even now, the mere touch of her hand lifted his heavy spirit. "You really know how to make me feel better—you know that?"

"Yeah, well, I also know how to get you hurt. If it weren't for me, you wouldn't be lying here right now."

"If it weren't for you, I might not have learned to trust God again," he said. "Belle, you made me come alive. I didn't realize it, but I was walking and talking like any normal person, but I was spiritually dead inside. I'm working on my relationship with God, and I want to work on a relationship with *you*.

"What I'm trying to say is I'm head over heels in love with you."

A pink hue filled her cheeks, and she shoved a curl behind her ear. The gesture was adorable and it only made his heart soar with delight.

"I love you too, Jonah. But we have time. You don't have to quit your job. Don't do that for me."

She leaned forward and brushed his cheek with her fingertips. The smell of fire and ash lingered on her skin. "Take some time off to recoup and we can try a real date. Preferably one where someone isn't trying to kill us," she said.

He grinned. "I'd like that, but that's what I'm trying to tell you. With my job, it's never as simple as that. I've never been able to do those things without risking someone seeing us and either blowing my cover or worse." He shook his head. "I refuse to put your life at risk like that, and that's why I'm done."

"Jonah—"

"Belle, what I mean is I'm done with undercover work. After everything with Malachi, my face will be in every newspaper across the country. I can't hide anymore."

She blinked. "So, not done with the FBI?"

"We'll see." He laughed.

He caressed her hand with his thumb. "You're right,

though. I need some time off. I need to work some things out with God. Let go of my guilt and start living my life."

"I understand." Her voice dipped and she looked at their hands.

Oh, he was making a mess of things. Why did it have to be so difficult? He should come right out and say it.

"Belle, what I'm trying to say is I want more than just a date. You're worth more to me than my job, especially if it keeps me away from you."

Her head snapped up and her eyes met his. "Are you sure?"

"Yes. Chase said the FBI has enough evidence for federal indictments on some key members of the drug cartel. The US Attorney will offer each one a plea agreement in exchange for the names of everyone involved with the organization. The undercover operation is over."

"What does that mean for *us*?"

"Well, I know it hasn't been long, but Belle, you make me want to be a better man. A Godly man. One who earns your trust and keeps it. I want to protect you, and learn everything about you, and then keep learning and pursuing your heart day after day."

The corners of her mouth lifted with each word he spoke until she beamed. There was something about her smile he found irresistible. The spark behind her blue eyes enraptured him and drew him in.

With his free hand he pressed the incline button on the hospital bed. The motor whirred as the bed raised him closer to Belle. It wasn't the most romantic move, but it did the trick. They were close now. Inches apart.

"You know, if I wasn't in so much pain, I'd take you in my arms and hold you for as long as you'd let me," he murmured.

Belle leaned forward, their noses nearly touching. "Is that the only thing stopping you?"

He shook his head and tried to think of the right words to match her wit. "I think…I think I'd like to—"

Belle bent and pressed her lips to his. A jolt of electricity shot through him, and he closed his eyes to savor the moment. All words forgotten, he cupped her head in his hands and deepened their kiss. Belle slipped her hand up and caressed his jaw.

Despite how much he wanted to continue, he broke the kiss. He stroked her hair, careful of the stitches on her forehead. He could get lost in her blue eyes and gorgeous smile.

"Kiss me again," she whispered.

And he did.

EPILOGUE

Eight Months Later

Belle shook her hands and blew out a breath. She could do this. Fifteen minutes of her life doing the thing she feared most. Piece of cake. A simple acceptance speech. How hard could it be?

Today, she would receive an award for her ground-breaking discovery of a new genus of conjugating green algae. The prestigious award came with millions in grant money for the university. A new laboratory was already in the works, but she still preferred her quiet work at the alpine lakes near her new home in Piney Village.

Belle peeked around the stage curtain. The size of the crowd stirred the butterflies in her stomach. Her pulse hammered and her mouth went dry. Why had she ever agreed to do this? A colleague had offered to accept on her behalf, but Belle summoned the courage to be here in person.

Eyes darting over the audience, she breathed a sigh of relief when she saw familiar faces. Colleagues and students from the university where she worked. Stella with Annie, Chase and Sheriff Riley.

And Jonah.

His warm smile eased her nerves. Their eyes met and

he crooked his index finger in a tiny wave. She smiled and blew him a kiss.

The audience erupted into applause, and she realized the master of ceremonies had announced her name. On wobbly legs, she took careful steps across the stage. Shook hands and accepted the glass award. After posing for several photographs, Belle positioned herself behind the podium. The applause died down.

Belle took a deep breath and launched into her acceptance speech. To her surprise, she sailed through with ease. After the award ceremony, a few investors approached with questions about her organic sunscreen. It seemed the scientific community wasn't alone in their excitement about her work.

Jonah slipped his arm around her waist. "You were amazing. I'm so proud of you, Belle."

The nickname stuck even after her memories returned. And she had to admit, she rather liked it. It represented the new her. New home in Piney Village. New friends. And…a new love.

She turned to face Jonah and planted a soft kiss on his lips. "Thank you for coming. It means the world to me."

"I'm glad I could be here," he said.

Belle released Jonah. They walked hand-in-hand to the exit and ducked outside. A gentle breeze chased them across the parking lot. "Are we on for dinner at Stella's tonight?"

"Sure are. Unless you're not up for it?"

"Wouldn't miss it."

Jonah opened the passenger door for her. She stood on her tiptoes and gave him a kiss before sliding into her seat.

They rode in silence until Jonah turned off the highway and began the long drive up the mountain to Piney Village.

"How did things go with Malachi this morning?"

Jonah exhaled. "Still refuses to see me."

Belle massaged his shoulder. "Keep trying. He might change his mind."

"I thought his guilty plea meant he was ready to move on. Make amends. At least have a relationship." Jonah shrugged. "Turns out he's incapable of letting anyone get close to him."

"In time, things could change."

He flashed a weak smile. "That's what I'm praying for. I know he's a killer, but he's the only blood relative I have left. I hope we can talk face-to-face one day. Even if it's through the prison bars."

"Well, he saved us from testifying, and I, for one, am thankful. He could've forced us to suffer a lengthy trial."

Jonah nodded. His shoulders sagged under the weight of everything they'd gone through.

Belle decided to change the subject. "How are you liking your new role in the FBI?"

"I love it, and I love how God orchestrated it. If we hadn't met, I don't know if I'd have thought to move into counterintelligence."

The FBI counterintelligence department had opened a case based on Belle's claims that Dr. Robert Winn stole her biofuel research. The investigation revealed Dr. Winn not only committed fraud, but he'd been communicating with some dangerous foreign adversaries, offering to sell trade secrets. Though Jonah had to travel some, he was able to make his base in Piney Village.

"Take it from me," Belle said. "We need FBI Counterintelligence to prevent theft of patents and research from universities. Your new job is invaluable to scientists like me."

Jonah turned off the main road to Piney Village and onto a rough gravel road. Belle looked around. The scenery was familiar, but she couldn't place where they were. A knot formed in her stomach. Why didn't she remember?

"Uh...Jonah?" Her voice vibrated along with the entire truck rumbling over the bumpy road. "Where are we?"

"You'll see in about three minutes." His eyes twinkled.

The truck rounded a corner and Belle gasped. Mountain peaks created a scenic backdrop for an expansive field of blossoming yellow-and-purple wildflowers. Rolling hills gave way to a small valley with a pristine lake at the center. The retreating spring sun painted the sky with hues of pink and purple that reflected off the lake like a mirror.

"Jonah, this place is gorgeous," she breathed. "How did you find it?"

"I thought you'd like it. It's called Big Fish Lake. Owned by a rancher friend of mine. He said we could use it anytime we'd like." Jonah pierced her with a knowing smile. "Even for research."

Belle returned the smile and studied the lake. The shoreline loop appeared to be a gentle hike of about three or four miles. Perfect for testing her hybrid algae.

Jonah parked his truck in a grassy area near a foot trail.

"Come on—I've packed us a snack." He reached behind the seat and produced a blue-and-yellow-checked blanket and an old-fashioned picnic basket.

The romantic gesture caused the butterflies in her belly to return. This day was getting better and better.

She held the basket while Jonah flicked the blanket through the air. It fluttered to the ground in a soft wave, and they settled beside each other. Jonah pulled the picnic basket closer.

"What's on the menu?" she asked.

"Ah, that's another surprise." He opened the lid and

began pulling out items. "I have two glasses. A bottle of sparkling grape cider. Smoked salmon with some water crackers. And this…"

In the palm of his hand, Jonah held a tiny velvet box. The diamond ring glittered and sparkled in the soft sunlight. Belle brought both hands to her mouth and gaped. Warmth spread throughout her chest and tears pricked her eyes. "Oh, Jonah…"

"We've been dating for several months now, but I've known since the first week we met that I wanted to spend the rest of my life with you. My love for you has only deepened the more I've come to know you."

He rose onto one knee and took her hand. Kissed the back. "Dr. Belinda Lewis, will you marry me?"

Belle flung her arms around his neck and kissed him. Her heart thudded and electricity crackled beneath her skin. He slipped his hand behind her head and deepened their kiss. Goose bumps shot up her arms.

When they parted, she sighed.

"Jonah Phillips, I love you with all my heart. Yes, I will marry you. A thousand times, yes. But only on one condition."

Confusion flashed behind his eyes. "Condition? What's the condition?"

She beamed a smile. "Call me Belle."

Jonah tossed his head and laughed. He dropped beside her and pulled her under his arm. "Anything for you…Belle."

* * * * *

Dear Reader,

Thank you for reading Belle and Jonah's story. I'm blessed to share my debut Love Inspired Suspense novel with you!

I developed the idea for this story while reading scientific articles about algae research. Yeah, I know. I'm a huge nerd. I thought a phycologist heroine would be intriguing and set about "meeting" Belle. After I'd submitted the synopsis for this story, my husband introduced me to his dear friend Bob. Over lunch one afternoon, we found ourselves discussing phycology—the study of algae. As it turns out, Bob is a phycologist! Isn't it fascinating how God brought us together at the right time?

Belle and Jonah learned that life can throw some curveballs, and they aren't always welcomed. But God orchestrated events to bring Belle and Jonah together, heal their wounds, and in the end, He gave them a happily-ever-after. So the next time life throws you a curveball, continue to seek and trust God knowing that He can straighten things out.

I'd love to keep in touch and hear your thoughts on this book so if you'd like, stop by my website www.kateangelo. com and send me a message. While you're there, don't forget to subscribe to my newsletter so you can hear all about my new releases.

Blessings,
Kate Angelo

COMING NEXT MONTH FROM
Love Inspired Suspense

UNDERCOVER OPERATION
Pacific Northwest K-9 Unit • by Maggie K. Black

After three bloodhound puppies are stolen, K-9 officer Asher Gilmore and trainer Peyton Burns are forced to go undercover as married drug smugglers to rescue them. But infiltrating the criminals will be more dangerous than expected, putting the operation, the puppies and their own lives at risk.

TRACKED THROUGH THE WOODS
by Laura Scott

Abby Miller is determined to find her missing FBI informant father before the mafia does, but time is running out. Can she trust special agent Wyatt Kane to protect her from the gunmen on her trail, to locate her father—and to uncover an FBI mole?

HUNTED AT CHRISTMAS
Amish Country Justice • by Dana R. Lynn

When single mother Addison Johnson is attacked by a hit man, she learns there's a price on her head. Soon it becomes clear that Isaiah Bender—the bounty hunter hired to track her down for crimes she didn't commit—is her only hope for survival.

SEEKING JUSTICE
by Sharee Stover

With her undercover operation in jeopardy, FBI agent Tiandra Daugherty replaces her injured partner with his identical twin brother, Officer Elijah Kenyon. But saving her mission puts Elijah in danger. Can Tiandra and her K-9 keep him alive before he becomes the next target?

RESCUING THE STOLEN CHILD
by Connie Queen

When Texas Ranger Zane Adcock's grandson is kidnapped and used as leverage to get Zane to investigate an old murder case, he calls his ex-fiancée for help. Zane and retired US marshal Bliss Walker will risk their lives to take down the criminals...and find the missing boy before it's too late.

CHRISTMAS MURDER COVER-UP
by Shannon Redmon

After Detective Liz Burke finds her confidential informant dead and interrupts the killer's escape, she's knocked unconscious and struggles to remember the details of the murder. With a target on her back, she must team up with homicide detective Oz Kelly to unravel a deadly scheme—and stay alive.

LOOK FOR THESE AND OTHER LOVE INSPIRED BOOKS WHEREVER BOOKS ARE SOLD, INCLUDING MOST BOOKSTORES, SUPERMARKETS, DISCOUNT STORES AND DRUGSTORES.

LISCNM0823

Get 3 FREE REWARDS!

We'll send you 2 FREE Books plus a FREE Mystery Gift.

FREE Value Over **$20**

Both the **Love Inspired®** and **Love Inspired®** Suspense series feature compelling novels filled with inspirational romance, faith, forgiveness and hope.

YES! Please send me 2 FREE novels from the Love Inspired or Love Inspired Suspense series and my FREE gift (gift is worth about $10 retail). After receiving them, if I don't wish to receive any more books, I can return the shipping statement marked "cancel." If I don't cancel, I will receive 6 brand-new Love Inspired Larger-Print books or Love Inspired Suspense Larger-Print books every month and be billed just $6.49 each in the U.S. or $6.74 each in Canada. That is a savings of at least 16% off the cover price. It's quite a bargain! Shipping and handling is just 50¢ per book in the U.S. and $1.25 per book in Canada.* I understand that accepting the 2 free books and gift places me under no obligation to buy anything. I can always return a shipment and cancel at any time by calling the number below. The free books and gift are mine to keep no matter what I decide.

Choose one:
☐ **Love Inspired Larger-Print** (122/322 BPA GRPA)
☐ **Love Inspired Suspense Larger-Print** (107/307 BPA GRPA)
☐ **Or Try Both!** (122/322 & 107/307 BPA GRRP)

Name (please print)

Address   Apt. #

City   State/Province   Zip/Postal Code

Email: Please check this box ☐ if you would like to receive newsletters and promotional emails from Harlequin Enterprises ULC and its affiliates. You can unsubscribe anytime.

Mail to the Harlequin Reader Service:
IN U.S.A.: P.O. Box 1341, Buffalo, NY 14240-8531
IN CANADA: P.O. Box 603, Fort Erie, Ontario L2A 5X3

Want to try 2 free books from another series? Call 1-800-873-8635 or visit www.ReaderService.com.

*Terms and prices subject to change without notice. Prices do not include sales taxes, which will be charged (if applicable) based on your state or country of residence. Canadian residents will be charged applicable taxes. Offer not valid in Quebec. This offer is limited to one order per household. Books received may not be as shown. Not valid for current subscribers to the Love Inspired or Love Inspired Suspense series. All orders subject to approval. Credit or debit balances in a customer's account(s) may be offset by any other outstanding balance owed by or to the customer. Please allow 4 to 6 weeks for delivery. Offer available while quantities last.

Your Privacy—Your information is being collected by Harlequin Enterprises ULC, operating as Harlequin Reader Service. For a complete summary of the information we collect, how we use this information and to whom it is disclosed, please visit our privacy notice located at corporate.harlequin.com/privacy-notice. From time to time we may also exchange your personal information with reputable third parties. If you wish to opt out of this sharing of your personal information, please visit readerservice.com/consumerschoice or call 1-800-873-8635. **Notice to California Residents**—Under California law, you have specific rights to control and access your data. For more information on these rights and how to exercise them, visit corporate.harlequin.com/california-privacy.

LIRLIS23

HARLEQUIN
PLUS

Try the best multimedia subscription service for romance readers like you!

Read, Watch and Play.

Experience the easiest way to get the romance content you crave.

Start your **FREE TRIAL** at
www.harlequinplus.com/freetrial.

HARPLUS0123